# IT ALL STARTED WITH A

# DARE

*A Novella*

# IT ALL STARTED WITH A DARE

Book Cover Designed: Debraj Saha
Editor(s): Emily
ISBN: 978-1-966672-09-8

Norris Imprint LLC

NORRIS IMPRINT

# IT ALL STARTED WITH A

# DARE

*A Novella*

## A.B. HOLTON

NORRIS IMPRINT

*For Amber and Sabria*

*"What begins as a dare may be fate's way of nudging you towards someone you never realized you needed."*

– A.B. Holton, *It All Started With A Dare.*

# Prologue

**"T**ruth or dare?" The voice brought her back to the present.

Her heart raced as she looked at the shaggy-haired guy grinning at her from across the circle. The room had gone quiet, and every pair of eyes was locked on her.

"Dare," she answered, surprising herself with the conviction of her voice.

A collective gasp and murmur rippled through the group, a surprised look plastered on their faces. The guy's grin widened, his expression devilish.

"I dare you to sleep with Stefan Jackson."

Laughter and gasps erupted, but Abby was deaf to it all. Her entire world had shrunk to a single point—the boy across the room who now sat straighter, his gaze fixed on her.

Stefan raised an eyebrow, his lips curling into a deliberate half-smile that oozed with the kind of confidence that made you ponder what he was planning.

She could feel her roommates' eyes on her, their whispers of encouragement going through one ear and out the other. Her grip tightened on her cup as she scrambled to come up with excuses, escape routes, and what this moment would mean.

She could say no, drink, and let the moment pass, retreating into her world of rules and predictability.

But when Stefan's smirk deepened, a flicker of curiosity sparked in his eyes, something shifted inside her.

For once in her life, Abby McKenna didn't want to be the girl who played it safe.

"I'll do it," she affirmed.

Stefan stood up from the couch, making his way toward her with slow, deliberate steps.

"You sure about this?" he asked, his gaze locking onto hers.

Abby swallowed hard but didn't look away. "I'm sure."

His grin faded, replaced by a deeper, more thoughtful look. He extended his hand.

And just like that, Abby McKenna stepped out of her comfort zone and into the unknown.

# Abby

"Come on, Abby! You move faster than this when you're late for class—you're practically Speedy Gonzales," Jessica shouted over the thundering bass that shook the frat house. Laughter and the chant of "chug, chug, chug" echoed from the partygoers, followed by the unmistakable smell of beer and other alcohol. Red Solo cups were the evening's hottest accessory—everyone had one, as if it was part of the dress code. I hovered at the entrance of the living room, my fingers nervously twisting the hem of my oversized cobalt sweater, feeling as out of place as a librarian at a rave.

You're probably wondering why I willingly walked into a place I've expertly avoided for three years. The answer is simple: Alexis and Jessica, my roommates and part-time life coaches, decided it was their mission to drag me here. They swore up and down it would be 'fun' and a 'necessary college experience,' as if beer pong were some academic requirement. Historically, I've been pretty good at dodging their persuasive tactics, but they've leveled up. So, here I am—reluctantly caving, mostly because I knew that if I didn't, I'd spend the next decade wondering if I missed out on something life-altering (Spoiler, probably not). I've never been the party type—in fact, I'm not even sure what type I am anymore. Is 'the type who regrets this already' a thing?

"Loosen up, McKenna," Jessica said, shoving a cup of suspiciously neon liquid into my hand. "You're young, you're hot, and tonight, you're living."

"I'm fine," I lied, gripping the cup like it might explode if I let go. My hand trembled, betraying me faster than my poker face ever could.

"Fine is boring," Alexis chimed in, giving me a playful nudge that sent me teetering toward the center of the room. "Come on, they're starting a game of Truth, Dare, or Drink. You *have* to play."

My first instinct was to bolt right out of there, but I didn't, so here I am sitting cross-legged on the sticky hardwood floor, surrounded by strangers who probably didn't even know my name.

The game kicked off, and with each turn, the dares became progressively more outrageous—like someone had secretly hired a chaos coordinator. And there I was, smack in the middle of it all, wondering what life choices had led me to this moment.

When the bottle spun and landed on me, it was like the universe had decided to put me in the spotlight. Every eye in the room turned toward me with the precision of synchronized swimmers. "You've got to be kidding me," I muttered. My cheeks burned, but I somehow managed to lift my gaze, meeting a sea of curious stares from strangers and the overly enthusiastic grins of Alexis and Jessica, who appeared like proud stage moms at a talent show.

"Truth or dare?" asked a shaggy-haired senior with a dramatic pause. The question filled the room with suspense as the players awaited my answer with bated breath.

"Dare," I blurted out before my brain could intervene. Instantly, my stomach somersaulted, and my voice wobbled. Putting on a show for everyone, I plastered on a brave face, which drew cheers from the group.

Across the circle, Mason—the apparent king of this chaos and owner of the party—grinned like the devil himself had whispered in his ear.

"I dare you to sleep with Stefan Jackson."

"What?!" I sputtered, my jaw almost hitting the sticky floor.

The circle erupted in gasps, popping like kernels in a microwave. My stomach dropped. I didn't need to ask who Stefan Jackson was—everyone knew him.

And there he was, lounging across the room like he owned the place. Stefan raised a single eyebrow, his lips curving into a slow, deliberate smile that screamed trouble. His brown skin glowed under the dim light, and a hint of stubble framed his sharp jawline. The confidence in his gaze was unnerving, as if he already knew my answer before I opened my mouth.

"Or you could drink," Mason says nonchalantly with a shrug, like he didn't just dare me to walk into the lion's den.

The cup in my hand felt as if it weighed a thousand pounds, its neon contents sloshing dangerously close to the rim as if mocking my indecision. A torrent of thoughts ran through my mind. Option one: drink and cement my reputation as the embodiment of predictability. Option two: choose truth and likely reveal my deepest, darkest secret. Option three: accept the dare—a night with Stefan Jackson, the playboy of the university and the walking definition of temptation.

It wasn't like I had anything to lose. Who was I kidding? Of course, I did. My track record of life choices reads like a manual for playing it safe: cautious, calculated, and about as thrilling as campus during the holiday break. Abby McKenna didn't take risks. But tonight, sitting on a sticky floor surrounded by strangers and under the intense scrutiny of Stefan's smoldering gaze, I couldn't help but wonder... what if I did?

"Sure," I said. The circle fell so silent you could've heard a pin drop. Then came the reactions: half the circle exploded into raucous cheers and whoops loud enough to rival the loud music, while the other half—mostly girls-shot daggers with their eyes, their disapproval evident.

Alexis and Jessica were no help either. "Girl, this is your chance!" Alexis whispered in my ear. "Go get him!?"

Jessica snorted, her grin nearly splitting her face. 'Geez, he looks like he's about to devour you whole,' she said as Stefan stood up from the couch. His gaze locked on me like a predator sizing up its prey.

Meanwhile, I sat there, trying not to explode from fear and awkwardness, which was visibly apparent. If only they knew I was mentally drafting my obituary.

"You coming?" he asked.

"Y-yeah," I croaked as I wobbled to my feet.

"That's my boy! Go get some!" Mason hollered, because of course he did. Stefan strode toward the stairs with a confidence that suggested he owned not just the party but possibly the entire zip code.

As I followed, my hand clutched the banister as if it were my last lifeline; a wave of trepidation hit me so hard that I nearly turned back. This was a bad idea—a catastrophic, what-was-I-thinking kind of idea. Yet the thought of retreating, of being branded a coward in front of this crowd, felt worse. My pride wouldn't allow it. Besides, I told myself that I would break free from the shackles of my comfort zone.

Although I'm starting to think my comfort zone wasn't so bad after all.

Here I stood unsteadily on the edge of that very promise where my pride and better judgment were battling like two boxers in a title match. Update: Pride was winning. In the end, the fleeting encounter with Stefan Jackson was irresistible.

"You don't have to go through with this," he said, his casual tone almost making me believe I had a choice. He pushed open the door to an empty room and glanced back at me with an infuriatingly calm expression. "You look like you're about to lose it. No pressure—we can stay here. Everyone will forget about this by tomorrow."

It's easy for him to say. He wasn't the one battling his moral compass over a terrible decision while trying not to back down. The rational part of me screamed to retreat, but then again, when has rationality ever made for a good story?

I stepped into the room, and he pulled a blunt from his jacket, slipping it between his lips as he leaned casually against the doorway as if he were starring in an indie film. It was surprisingly decent of him to offer me an out, but my pride wasn't about to let me take it. I took a shaky breath, fully aware of my questionable life choices. I could easily take the easy way out, but…

"I want to," I said.

His eyes locked onto mine as he stepped into the room, shutting the door behind him with a soft click that somehow sounded louder than my heartbeat. The only light came from the glowing red tip of his blunt, casting flickering shadows across his face. I wondered what I had just signed up for.

## Chapter Two

## Abby

"**A**re you sure?" he asked again, closing the space between us. Instinctively, I stepped back, landing on the edge of the bed with all the grace I could muster.

My lips quivered. 'Y-yeah,' I managed to say.

It had been years—literal years—since I'd experienced anything close to intimacy, and my body was craving attention. Stefan gave me a slow once-over that made me feel both seen and entirely undone. With a flick of his fingers, he snuffed out his blunt, his cocky smile widening as he leaned in and pushed me gently down onto the bed.

I yelped and swallowed, watching as he slowly climbed onto the bed. His precision moves and confidence suggested this wasn't his first rodeo. His knee slid between my thighs, nudging them apart, sending my skirt riding up in surrender. He leaned down, his face hovering just inches from mine.

"First time?" he asked.

His breath grazed my skin, and I became intoxicated by the sweet, pungent aroma of the grape-flavored blunt he'd been smoking. My heart pumped quickly, and I found myself panting softly.

"N-no," But it's… It's been a while,' I stammered.

"Is that a problem?"

"No, not a problem," he says. His fingers trail up my throat and along my jawline, causing a shiver to run down my spine. He continues as his tongue flicks across my fingers. My brain short-circuited somewhere between what was *happening and a plea not to stop.*

Stefan's hands slid up my sides, pausing just below my shoulder blades, and suddenly, my body began to overheat like an old car on a summer day. A hum escaped my lips before I could swallow it. He smirked as if he had just won a bet.

"I haven't even done anything yet, and you're already squirming?" he whispered, his breath tickling my ear. Then his lips found my neck, slow and deliberate, leaving what I was sure would be a mark—a bold declaration of what happened.

In my defense, given how long it's been since I felt someone else's touch, I couldn't bring myself to care. If anything, I was ready to frame the bruise as a badge of honor.

He gradually lifted the hem of my sweater and pulled it over my head, allowing my breasts to spill out into the freezing night air. My arms instantly covered my breasts.

"Remove your hands," he said, which sounded like a command.

I obeyed, letting my hands fall to my sides as though I had just been caught red-handed committing an illegal act. I resisted the urge to cover myself and looked away, unable to maintain eye contact. Meanwhile, I shivered—not from the cold, but from the sheer anticipation.

He started to run his fingers down my breasts, passing over my nipple. My body got hotter; I could feel the wetness in my panties.

His fingers moved further down onto my stomach, dipped into my navel, and then traced lightly over my intimate area. I arched into his touch as moans escaped my lips.

He chuckled. "Does that feel good?" he asks. My face flushed, and I was unable to respond. I swallowed hard as he straddled me, pinning me completely against the bed.

"Arms up!" he demanded. I hesitated for a split second, then surrendered.

I bit my bottom lip in embarrassment at the exposure. Then I felt it—something tight wrapping around my wrists, binding them together. I glanced up and caught Stefan expertly tying them with some fabric, holding it to the headboard before securing it.

Panic surged through me as I felt the bite on my wrists, helpless to escape.

"Stefan—" I began to protest, but his lips silenced me.

"I'm not going to hurt you. Trust me, you'll enjoy it," he assured.

"Are you sure?"

"I promise you'll like it," he said, "but if you want to stop, we can."

I debated whether to make him stop or let him continue; in the end, I forced myself to remain calm. I lay stiffly, waiting for his next move.

In his hands, I was powerless, yet the thrill of that helplessness caused my body to quiver with excitement. He pulled at the fabric, testing their hold, and my heart thundered.

My eyes found him for the first time in a while, and his face was a picture of arousal.

"Look at you, all wrapped up like a gift just for me. You've never done this, huh?"

"I shook my head."

"I can tell." He teased. His voice was a low rumble that left a trail of goosebumps in its wake.

"Stefan."

"Yes."

I breathed; my voice a bit shaky, unsure of what to say. "Please," I begged quietly. He watched me with a predatory gaze as his signature smirk tugged at the corners of his lips. I thrust my lower body toward him, trying to gain some friction.

"Please, what? Tell me what you want, Angel?"

I gulped. He pulled away and unzipped his pants; it seemed as though he was moving in slow motion. Perhaps it was for his own good that my hands were tied because I might have jumped his bones by now. When his pants finally came off, my heart skipped a beat. I licked my lips, craving his touch.

"You should see yourself." He knelt at the edge of the bed; his eyes gleamed with delight as they roamed over my exposed body once more.

"The things I could do to you," he commented.

"Stefan," I groaned, wriggling against his mischief cuffs. His view of me must have been priceless. Every tug and twist made the fabric bite into my skin as if it had a personal vendetta.

"Impatient, are you?" he chuckled, positioning himself between my legs, spreading them, and staring unabashedly. His hands glided sensually over my thighs.

"You have no idea what's in store for you," Stefan murmured, his warm breath dancing against my inner thigh as he got closer. His teeth lightly grazed my skin, and the sensation made me tense in surprise. However, it was the wicked undertones that left me yearning for more.

"Hah—" The sound caught in my throat as I trembled with need.

My back arched naturally as his mouth moved lower down my body.

He took his time as his lips brushed over my pussy lips, each kiss a tantalizing tease that fueled my desire. I couldn't hold back the whimper that escaped my mouth.

"Beautiful," He remarked and licked his lips before he suddenly grabbed my thighs and almost bent me in half. I drew a sharp breath in shock, certain my face was red at the new position. I felt exposed before, but this was altogether unbelievable. Stefan held me effortlessly, the grip on my thighs both possessive and demanding.

"What a view." He said while he eyed me and licked his lips. What a cruel thing to do, he's such a tease. My breath quickened, and I was unguarded and utterly vulnerable. "Stefan…" I whimpered. "Don't worry, little Angel, I'll take care of you gorgeous," he said and squeezed my ass. It ignited a new wave of heat that pooled at the base of my feet. Then I felt a finger, "Stefan, please…" I wanted more, no, I needed more. "I need…ah!" I threw my head back when he suddenly added two fingers and pushed into my tight heat. I had no time to adjust as his fingers moved in and out of me, one arm still holding my legs in place.

"Ahh...fuck...yeah...right...there...yess fuck!" I moaned and pressed my head into the pillow while my back arched. My cries were rewarded with a third finger. I felt a slight sting as they stretched me open.

"Feels so good," I murmured. He rubbed against my wall, just slightly grazing the spot inside me that would make me see stars. His fingers pumped into me with force, moving my whole body.

My breath came in desperate pants as I stared up at him. My limbs felt heavy, a blend of exhaustion and desire.

He leaned back, grabbed my waist, and lifted it. I whimpered at the abrupt emptiness; the sensation of being so thoroughly exposed made me squirm. His hands gripped my thighs, firm yet gentle. I lay still in place like a bendable Barbie doll as he slid on a condom, too fast for me to process, and positioned himself against my entrance. I let out a soft whimper; my eyes were wide as I felt the pressure. My body tensed, and my heart thudded in my chest.

"Relax."

I took a deep breath, inhaled, and exhaled.

His next question was low and throaty, "Ready?" Caught off guard by a rush of feelings, I paused momentarily before nodding. The next second, I felt the pressure again, but this time, he didn't stop and entered me.

"Oh!" I exclaimed, gripping the fabric tightly.

"Are you okay?" he asked.

"It hurts."

"It'll feel good soon," he promised.

14

"Is it okay if I move?"

"Yes." I felt so full, and the pain was as if I were losing my virginity again.

The more he moved, the better it felt; I couldn't help but moan.

"Feels good, huh?" he asked before he rammed his cock back in me, which took my breath away. The force caused my body to be pushed up towards the headboard, and a satisfied groan left my lips.

"Yes...ah..." I nearly sobbed. Each thrust was so strong and precise that the pain now felt heavenly; my whole body grew numb. His rhythm picked up as he dove deeper into my core. The headboard creaked in protest.

"Look at you," he panted, his gaze fixated on my body. Every thrust sent me deeper into a state of blissful surrender. This felt nothing like my first time. I have never experienced anything like this before. I wanted to hold him close, run my fingers down his back and feel the dimples on his ass cheeks as he pounded into me.

"You like this," he grunted, rubbing my clit while pounding my pussy. My eyes rolled back as sensation upon sensation of pleasure spread through me. My body reacted instinctively, tightening around him, drawing out more of that delicious friction that left me dizzy and pleasured.

"Stefan... so good." I babbled as I tried to hold onto the fabric binding my wrists.

I gasped at the sudden loss of connection when he pulled out. I looked up at him as I tried to understand what happened when my body was suddenly turned around. My chest pressed against the sheets, and my wrists twisted. A rush of shock coursed through me as Stefan repositioned me. I felt excited. Heat radiated from my body. My hips were pulled up until I was on my knees. My head was pressed into the pillow because I couldn't hold myself up on my arms. I turned my head to see where Stefan was.

"Perfect," I heard him mumble before he pushed back inside me, taking me from behind as if nothing else mattered. The forceful thrusts of his cock caused me to scream.

"Oh!" I moaned and moaned as Stefan claimed me completely, pushing deeper than before. My senses were ablaze; my body quaked as I yielded to the blissful surrender of being filled by him.

When he hit my sensitive spot, I bit down on my lips to keep my voice down, more aware of the party downstairs than ever. I sobbed in pure ecstasy.

"Shit, you're so fucking tight," he growled. I felt a sharp pain when his hand smacked against my ass, eliciting a pleased hum. I never knew that I liked being spanked, but thanks to him, a lot of myself was being revealed to me. He gave me what I wanted. His thrusts got faster and harder; his hands massaged my ass before another slap landed on my other cheek.

His hand found its way into my hair and pulled my head back. My eyes clenched shut as I breathed out. "Ah, I'm...close...ah."

He grunted and hastened his pace; it only took a few more thrusts before pleasure swept away every coherent thought. "Stefan!" I cried out. My eyes rolled back in my head as I sobbed from the intensity of my orgasm, but he didn't stop and continued pounding into me, prolonging my climax.

He had a pleased look on his face while his body went taut. He moaned, and his hips stuttered as he came, spilling into the condom. I panted and felt my body going through the aftershocks. I didn't even process when he began to loosen up the binds, too fucked out to.

I vaguely heard Stefan laugh as he propped me onto the bed properly. "Get some sleep, you'll need it." My eyes began to close, and before I realized it, I was too blissed out to care about anything else.

# *Chapter Three*

## Abby

I couldn't get out of there fast enough. The morning sun felt like a spotlight on my face, as if it knew all my secrets. I weaved through campus, dodging the last stragglers still stumbling home from the party. I kept my head down, fingers gripping the strap of my bag. Last night? A fever dream. The dare. Stefan. His cocky smirk, his touch, his… Nope. Abort mission. I shook my head so hard that I probably looked like I was trying to dislodge a bee. No indecent thoughts today, brain. Not on my watch.

By the time I reached our dorm, I could already hear Alexis and Jessica's voices wafting from the kitchen. They'd be waiting, no doubt armed with a million questions, ready to pounce. And me? I had nothing coherent to offer. What was I supposed to say? That I'd just had the kind of mind-blowing sex that rewired my brain? Yeah, that would go over well.

I swung the door open and breezed past Alexis and Jessica like I hadn't just detonated a drama bomb. 'Abby!' Alexis called, but I wasn't about to stop for an interrogation. Instead, I retreated to my room and flopped onto my bed. Last night had been... well, unforgettable. Embarrassing? Absolutely. Regret-worthy? Not even close. If anything, it was the kind of memory that would make me blush for years.

Exhaustion permeated my entire day. I sleptwalked through classes and conversations; I couldn't help myself after that night. I tried, with great effort, to push thoughts of him out of my mind and focus on school. But my mind was stubbornly fixated on the events of the previous night. Those memories haunted me, refusing to release their grip on my thoughts. I wondered why that night was so impossible to forget.

As I approached my final lecture, I felt a sense of relief. The prospect of returning home had never seemed so appealing. At least this way, I could reminisce comfortably without interruptions. But fate had other plans once again.

As I turned the corner near the lecture hall, my feet suddenly stopped moving. I blinked once, then twice, to confirm that I wasn't imagining things.

Stefan's appearance was as surprising as getting your period after being late. You're happy because it came, but the unexpectedness left you in a mess. There he was, casually leaning against the wall just outside the door, his tall frame impossible to miss. His signature smirk was already locked and loaded, aimed straight at me like he'd been waiting for this exact moment. My stomach flipped like a gymnast at the Olympics. I hadn't expected to see him here today of all days, in this way of all ways. Honestly, I didn't expect to see him ever again, but maybe that's just my flair for the dramatic talking.

"McKenna,' he called, a glint lighting up his eyes. 'What's the matter? Couldn't wait to run away from me?"

I blinked, frozen, unable to move. My mouth was drier than a terrible open mic night, and my palms were slightly clammy.

"W-what?" I croaked.

He pushed off the wall and took a step toward me; with each step closer, the hallway seemed to shrink.

"You heard me," he said.

My brain? Completely offline. What was I supposed to say to that? Come on, think, think, think, I mentally screamed at myself, but my thoughts were playing hide-and-seek. My pulse quickened, and suddenly every nerve in my body was hyper-aware of him.

Oh God, his scent. It's earthy, think woodsy, and impossibly clean. I inhaled sharply, and it was like a sensory ambush. He was too close now, so close that I could feel the heat radiating off him. My mouth went dry as my brain continued its unhelpful silence. If I didn't say something soon, this hallway was going to swallow me whole—or worse, he'd know just how much power he had over me.

"Stefan, I..." I started to say, but the damn words dissolved faster than sugar in hot tea. My brain had officially checked out, leaving me stranded in awkward silence.

"Before I could figure out how to salvage the moment, he leaned in—just enough to make my breath hitch. His nose brushed through my hair as he inhaled, and I swear my knees almost gave out.

"You smell amazing."

Is he trying to turn me into a puddle? Because if that's the plan, it's working. His compliment tugged a smile from me, and the warmth of his breath on my neck sent goosebumps across my skin.

My heart pounded so hard it felt like I'd just sprinted a mile at full speed. I instinctively stepped back, his eyes flicked to my face, and I swear he could hear my heart racing. He smiled—a slow, knowing smile—and said, "I'll be seeing you," his voice dipping an octave like he was sharing some delicious secret meant only for me.

I was sweating in places I shouldn't, my cheeks reddened, and I couldn't even look at him, so I stared at the floor, pretending it had suddenly become fascinating. With that, he walked away.

What just happened? "I'll be seeing you"? What does that even mean? And why, for the love of all things sane, do I want to find out so badly?

I had just crawled out of an exhausting study session—midterms were approaching, and I was determined to be as prepared as humanly possible. These tests, along with finals, were my last hurdles before the grand march across the graduation stage. I was doing everything right: reading every chapter, drowning in notes, and following my color-coded schedules.

And yet, despite all my efforts, my brain kept circling back to Stefan. He is my biggest distraction. Here I was, trying to conquer midterms, and he'd somehow taken up permanent residence in my head.

Deciding I deserved a break (and maybe a little reward for surviving this long), I made my way to the kitchen in search of a drink and a snack.

"Abby, are you alive back there?" Alexis called from the living room.

"Yeah, yeah, I'm here," I replied, dragging myself toward the living room. Alexis was sprawled across the couch like a soldier fallen in battle, her textbooks scattered around her. Her phone buzzed angrily on the coffee table, and she looked one missed call away from a full-blown meltdown.

"What's going on?" I inquired.

"Ugh, I can't take this anymore!" she groaned dramatically, chucking a book onto the floor like it had personally offended her. "I'm so dumb."

"Now you know that's not true," I said, dodging a flying highlighter as she flailed her arms in frustration.

"Then why can't I grasp this stupid concept?" she wailed.

"Alexis, you are one of the most intelligent people I know, and I'm not just saying that because we are friends. I mean it."

Her eyes narrowed suspiciously before softening into a small smile. "Do you really think that?"

"I know that much."

She sighs and flops back onto the couch in distress. "I'm drowning in case law, Abby. How am I supposed to study all this nonsense and have a life?!"

I plopped down beside her and surveyed all the textbooks, notes, and highlights she'd created. "It's not easy," I said sympathetically, though honestly, I had no idea how to help. My expertise in pep talks was limited to offering snacks and vague encouragement.

"You should take a break," I suggested. "Get some fresh air, clear your head, and then tackle it again."

She rubbed her temples, her braids piled into a messy high bun. "You're right," she sighs again.

"I can't endure this any longer."

I handed her a bottle of wine cooler as if it were a peace offering.

She eyed it and snorted. "Girl, I'm gonna need something way stronger than this." We both burst out laughing because, honestly, same.

Then, out of nowhere, she sat up straight like she'd just had an epiphany. "Let's go out!" she declared.

"Or," I countered cautiously, "we could relax right here or maybe on the patio? Fresh air is right outside the door."

She rolled her eyes so hard I was surprised they didn't get stuck. "Seriously, Abby? I need a real change of scenery. Let's hit the club! A drink or two, some terrible dance moves, and a few hours of forgetting this mess ever existed—sounds perfect. Come on, what do you say? Are you in?"

I opened my mouth, ready to unleash my usual excuses: I'm not a club person. It's too loud, too chaotic, too… everything. But I stopped myself. Alexis looked like she needed this—a mental reset to scrape law off her brain and regroup.

"Please," she whined, dragging out the word like a toddler begging for candy.

"Fine," I sighed, hauling myself to my feet. "But only one drink. And don't even think about getting me on the dance floor."

Her face lit up like she'd just won the lottery. "Deal!" she exclaimed, springing to her feet.

"Come on," she said with a mischievous grin, "let's find you something sexy to wear and get you out of that shell you're so fond of."

"This isn't 'getting out of my shell.' You and Jessica already cracked it open last week, remember?" I reminded her as we trudged upstairs to change.

"Where is Jess, anyway?" I asked, hoping to distract her from whatever outfit she was about to force on me.

"She's staying over at her friend's place tonight," which means it's just us—trust me, Abby, we're going all out.

# Chapter Four

## Abby

The club was just as I had pictured it—loud, with flashing lights that could easily trigger a migraine. All around were bodies swaying and gyrating shamelessly to the beat of the music. Alexis, of course, was in her element. She happily dragged me through the crowd. The change of scenery worked wonders for her mood; meanwhile, I felt like a fish flopping on dry land, wishing I could teleport back to my bed.

Not wanting to rain on Alexis's parade, I found a corner by the bar and claimed my spot.

The music was so loud that I had to lean over the counter and shout my order, "Sex on the Beach, please!" "Thanks!"

The bartender flashed a quick smile and got to work. A moment later, he handed me the drink. My fingers wrapped around it, but it didn't alleviate my awkwardness, nor did it provide the comfort I expected.

It wasn't until I saw him that I realized coming here might have been a terrible idea. Scratch that—it was a horrible idea.

Then again, lately, all my decisions seemed to fall somewhere between influenced and impulsive.

Stefan Jackson was impossible to miss, of course—his coils of brown curls shimmered under the club lights. His honey-bronzed skin radiated warmth, and those deep-set eyes? Oh, those deep, wondering eyes were inviting enough to make you forget your train of thought. If somehow you didn't notice all that, the gaggle of groupies around him would ensure that you did. They laughed far too hard at whatever he said, as if he had just delivered the punchline of the century. I tried to pull my gaze away, but then our eyes locked. Shit. My heart did something strange that I couldn't explain. The way he looked at me made everyone in the crowd fade into irrelevance.

There was a boyish charm in the curve of his lips that could get him out of parking tickets. Yet that damn signature devil-may-care smirk made you want to wipe it right off his alluring face.

His perfectly arched eyebrow lifted in a way that spelled trouble. My blood decided to go into overdrive, pumping furiously to keep up with my heart's frantic pace. I swallowed hard, suddenly hyper-aware of the ridiculous dress Alexis had stuffed me into.

Thanks to Alexis, I wore a form-fitting, slinky red dress with tiny straps that nearly made my breasts spill out. And now, with Stefan's eyes fixed on me, I felt even more exposed than I already was.

Where was Alexis, anyway? I tore my gaze away from him and spotted her on the dance floor, completely losing herself in the music. I had to give her credit: the girl could dance.

I, on the other hand, sipped my drink, pretending that the floating ice chips were the most fascinating thing in the room—anything to avoid his gaze and keep up my disappearing act.

"Hey, you look lost."

I looked up, startled, to see the culprit behind the interruption—a guy leaning against the bar. His friendly smile and charming face were enough to derail my thoughts and disrupt my performance of *"Invisible Girl "*with a single, casual sentence.

I took another swig of my drink and replied, "I'm not lost, but this isn't exactly my scene."

"Mind if I keep you company?" he asked. Before I could respond, I felt a strong and familiar presence beside me.

Stefan had appeared out of nowhere, his arm brushing mine in a way that sent sparks straight to my fingertips. "She's not interested," he said.

I turned to look at him, taken aback by his sudden intrusion but even more so by how the guy immediately backed off, hands raised in surrender as if Stefan had declared martial law.

"My bad. I didn't know she was your girl." I was about to say I wasn't his girlfriend, but Stefan's attention shifted back to me, his brown eyes holding me in place once more. His confidence was infuriating; I wanted to be annoyed by his interruption, but those sparks lingering on my skin made it hard to focus on anything else.

"Abby McKenna," he says, "I didn't expect to see you here. Already trying to erase me from your memory?"

My mouth opened, ready to fire back something clever and perhaps less awkward—yet my brain decided to take a mini break once more. So, I stood there, tongue-tied, while he looked at me as if he had all the time in the world. Something about how he enunciated my name as if he was savoring it made my heart beat a little faster.

"Maybe," I replied at last. "I just came out for a drink and a change of scenery."

His grin deepened, dangerously close to lethal territory. "Is that so?" he asked, leaning in slightly. "Do you mind if I steal some of your time then?"

Without my response, his fingers brushed against mine as he lifted my glass from my hand. The smooth move left me wondering if I was about to lose more than just my drink.

"Stefan—" I started to speak, but he took my hand in his. His skin was slightly rough, yet his touch was gentle; my hand fit perfectly in his. I almost forgot what I intended to say as he maneuvered through the crowd with purposeful strides.

"Wait!" I protested, stumbling into his back as he abruptly stopped. "I can't just leave—I came with my friend, Alexis."

He glanced at the dance floor, his expression focused. "She'll be fine. She's dancing with Kevin."

I quickly scanned the crowd, and sure enough, Alexis and Kevin were like stars in a music video. Sighing, I texted her to let her know I wasn't abandoning her to the wolves.

Stefan took my hand and led me outside without giving me a chance to overthink. We walked past the bouncers into the crisp night air. The pounding music from the club faded into the background, replaced by the hum of passing cars and the occasional honk.

It was quieter out here—almost too calm, as if the night was holding its breath. Without a word, Stefan pulled me closer, pressing me against his sleek black sports car as if it were part of his master plan. My heart thundered in my chest, working overtime as he closed the gap between us, his chest flush against mine, his warm breath teasing my skin.

"You look stunning in that dress," he says.

Then, with a mischievous glint, he added, "Honestly, you'd look alluring even in a trash bag."

The absurdity of the compliment and the heat in his gaze made me let out a soft moan before I could stop myself. His hands cupped my face with such gentleness that I felt trapped by the sheer gravity of his touch.

And then he kissed me. It wasn't just a kiss; it was the kind that made you forget your name.

It was unexpected but far from unwelcome. His lips were rough and moved with a deliberate intensity that left no room for hesitation. When I didn't pull away, he deepened the kiss; his hand slid to the small of my back and pulled me closer until there was no space between us. His taste was intoxicating— warm, heady, and utterly inescapable. Everything about him screamed danger, and yet I couldn't get enough. It was like he'd flipped some hidden switch inside me.

When we broke apart, I was breathless and hot all over. Stefan's eyes locked onto mine; a smile tugged at the corners of his lips.

"You good?" he teased.

I didn't trust my voice, so I nodded in acknowledgment.

Without another word, he opened the car door for me. I slid inside, still trying to catch my breath as he shut the door behind me, slipped into the driver's seat, and drove off into the night.

## Chapter Five

# Abby

We stumbled into what I assumed was his house. I had no time to take in my surroundings when Stefan's lips found mine, devouring me as if I were the last thing on his to-do list. His teeth nipped at my skin with an intensity that left me breathless and utterly helpless. The door slammed shut behind us, and my world was suddenly flipped upside down.

One moment, I was standing, and the next, I was hoisted over his shoulder like a sack of potatoes (albeit a very willing one). His hand stayed firmly planted on my ass as he carried me upstairs. He pushed open a door, and my heart raced as I heard the unmistakable click of it shutting behind us.

With zero time wasted, Stefan tossed my bag into the corner and lay me on his bed. My shoes hit the floor just a short time after. I took a second to regain my equilibrium—being flipped upside down will do that to you—but as soon as I did, my hands found their way to his abs. And oh, *what a discovery.*

Finally, touching him felt AMAZING. My tongue itched for a taste, so I clumsily unbuttoned his shirt and gave in to the urge, licking a line across his skin. It was salty but oddly satisfying. My teeth found his nipple, and I bit down gently; he took in a sharp intake of breath.

He groaned and pulled away, leaving me flushed. My skin felt like it was on fire, and my chest rose and fell rapidly as I tried to catch my breath. Stefan peeled off his shirt, letting it crumple in the corner of the room. His intense, deliberate eyes remained fixed on mine. As he reached to pull my dress, he suddenly paused.

"Are you drunk?" he inquired.

Confused by his sudden change, I shook my head. "No."

"I need to hear it," he said, his tone serious, eyes locked on mine. "Do you want to continue?"

A playful grin spread across my lips.

"I'm not drunk, and I want you to fuck me silly," I responded. *Who even am I right now?* I thought, startled by my boldness.

His lips curved into that signature devilish smirk. "That's exactly what I wanted to hear."

"Arms up," he instructed.

In one fluid motion, he stripped the dress from my body, leaving me exposed beneath his hungry gaze. Stefan lay on top of me, my body trapped between his strong thighs, which forced me to stay still as he took his time with my lips. He licked me, tasting me all over his mouth. His hand moved from my waist, his thumb rested on my chin, his fingers closed around my neck without exerting pressure, and he waited for confirmation. I nod breathlessly. "I need words, Angel," he said. I trembled beneath him.

"Yes, please," I panted.

Stefan groaned and tightened his grip around my neck, causing me to moan. I needed more. My nails scratched up his back as I craved more contact.

"S-Ste…fan," I whined when he loosened his grip on my neck, allowing air to flow back to me again.

"Abby," he mimicked me. His breath smelled like strawberries and alcohol. We locked eyes again. "Take off everything you're wearing," he commanded. I obeyed.

"You too," I retorted, removing my half-bra and panties.

Soon, we were both naked. I was unable to keep still; I needed him inside me already.

"Relax, Angel," he teased; he opened the drawer next to his bed and grabbed a condom. I blushed and looked away, embarrassed. "Don't be like that, Angel. I like it when you're eager for me." He smirked devilishly." My heart melts every time he calls me Angel. Even though I know better that this isn't real, I can't help it.

"You make me want to fuck you senseless," he said. A shiver runs through me at his crude words, and my heart begins to pound loudly in my chest.

I gripped the sheets, anxious as he kissed my chest, giving brief attention to my nipples, leaving them swollen with wet suction and kisses. He kissed down to my lady part, playing with my clit and blowing on it..

I gasped and arched against him. He turned me onto the bed and spread my legs. I was on all fours, fully exposed and dripping for him. For a moment, everything was silent. I waited for his touch, a finger, or anything. What I didn't expect was the wet and flexible touch against my vagina.

"Mmhhgh S-Stefan... You don't need to." I puff, too embarrassed and aroused. Stefan doesn't respond. He just continued the slow movement at my entrance, occasionally entering me with the tip of his tongue, which elicited more eager moans from my lips.

Finally, he pushed his tongue as far as he could inside me, and the sheer pressure made me try to close my legs, but he held my left leg in place, leaving me still exposed.

"Tasty," he said as he withdrew his tongue from inside me and gave a not-so-hard slap on my asscheeks.

"You..." "You didn't need to do that..." "My God, so embarrassing," I mumbled.

"You mean delicious." he goes down on me again, licking and slurping at my wet hole. When he inserted his fingers in me, a long, contented sigh escaped my lips, a sound of pure pleasure.

"Yeah, right there," I moaned, tilting my head back and grabbing a handful of his hair.

He doesn't wait long to start the scissoring movements to stretch me. I shivered at his touch.

"What do you want, Angel?" He asked.

My heart pumped faster, and my breath grew shorter; my body felt blissful.

"You," I whined. "Please fuck me." My words were plain desperate, and Stefan loved it. He put on the condom in record time and flipped me over to my back.

His hands were on either side of my head, holding his body above me. He had his cock, trying to balance, and began to push the head inside me. Stefan took all the time in the world; he went slowly and waited for me to get used to it, as he continued to kiss me, which distracted me from the pain. That had quickly been replaced with pleasure.

He finally bottomed out, and we let out simultaneous moans, panting at the feeling. After a while, he said, "I'm going to move, okay."

I nodded. Something about this time felt different, in a good way. It was more intimate. His kisses, touches, and words were perfect. It gave me butterflies and left me wondering what it would be like to be more than just sex. Maybe it's just my hormones talking. His fast thrusts brought me back to the moment. The noises our bodies produced were amplified throughout the room, and my wetness made the sounds even more obscene.

"Faster," I entreated pathetically; it must have excited him because soon he ran as deep as possible into me, and I felt his balls forcefully hit against my ass.

From then on, I was flipped, tossed, and spread in various positions; the room was filled with moans, groans, and his aggressive yet sensual, pleasurable thrusts that drove me crazy.

"You're so fucking hot, Holy shit," he rasped. "I want to fuck this tight pussy forever." "No one else but me." He kissed my heels as I moaned mindlessly beneath him.

"M-me too," I panted amidst the thrusts. "I'm almost...Stefan, I'm going to c-cum." I whimpered as I felt my orgasm near; my legs trembled.

My head fell back as I orgasmed. Stefan followed right after. There were tears in my eyes, and my entire body felt euphoric.

I took in every detail of Stefan as he came undone—the furrow of his brows, the way his slightly parted lips flushed red, his cheeks glowing with heat, and those closed, focused eyes that made him look vulnerable and captivating simultaneously. He was hot as fuck, and I couldn't take my eyes off him.

When he pulled out, I collapsed back onto the bed, completely spent. My body melted into the sheets, still high from our strenuous activity. Stefan followed, collapsing on top of me and kissing me passionately for a while.

We remained like that for a long time, only stopping to catch our breath. I felt the bed dip, and a little while later, something warm and damp pressed gently between my legs. The gesture touched me as I drifted off to sleep. My only wish was for this moment to last forever.

# Chapter Six

## Abby

Iwoke up to an unfamiliar ceiling. The delicate light of dawn lit up the room. It took me a few seconds to piece everything together—his bed, his clothes—*Stefan's house*. My heart jolted as I sat up; panic crept in. *Not again*. I told myself this wouldn't happen again, that it was a one-time thing. Yet here I was, tangled in his sheets like déjà vu.

I tried to make sense of it all, replaying the night in my head. How had I ended up here again? Was it impulsiveness? Weakness? Or was it simply Stefan, with his maddening charm and how he made me forget every carefully planned boundary I had established for myself?

I took a deep, prolonged breath and then released it to calm my racing heart. The sheets beneath my fingertips felt luxurious and expensive, as if they belonged in a five-star hotel, not wrapped around my current predicament. The scent of Stefan's cologne still enveloped me in a way that made me want to crawl back under the covers and snuggle close to him.

I heard distinct, nearby voices, and my whole body tensed. "Shit!" "*It must be his parents.*"

Suddenly, the soft sheets felt less inviting and more like a trap I needed to escape.

I had never met Stefan's parents, but knew who they were. Olivia Jackson wasn't just a fashion designer but a walking Vogue cover, constantly in the headlines for her jaw-dropping style and high-profile collaborations. Then there was Robert Jackson, a successful patent attorney who probably trademarked his son's signature smirk. Together, they were the kind of power couple you'd see in glossy magazines—polished and certainly not the sort of people I wanted to meet while sneaking out of their son's bedroom.

The thought of facing them in these circumstances made my stomach hurt. Just imagining Olivia's discerning designer eye assessing me made my skin crawl—or worse, Robert's lawyerly glare dissecting every poor decision that had brought me to this moment.

I scrambled out of bed, shaking my hands as I gathered the clothes Stefan had tossed aside the night before. The voices grew louder and clearer, causing my panic to rise.

I dressed at lightning speed. There was no graceful exit now, no sneaky escape route to save me from this impending disaster. The longer I stayed in this unfamiliar place, the more awkward it became. I took a deep breath, summoned every ounce of courage I had left—admittedly not much—and stepped out of the bedroom. My only prayer? To survive this without collapsing from nerves or embarrassment.

The living room was as elegant as I'd imagined—tasteful, minimalist furniture accented by pops of color, like the bold yellow chair and the chrome coffee table stacked with artfully arranged books and magazines. The whole room smelled like *money.* Not that this was the time for an HGTV-style tour, but can you blame me? Last night, I'd been too busy getting lost in Stefan's kisses to appreciate it earlier.

"Stay focused!" I hissed at myself, snapping out of my interior design daydream. My eyes darted to the door and then back to the kitchen. Could I make a break for it? Maybe if I moved quickly enough or if I could teleport, it would come in handy right now. I could vanish without a trace.

Before I could even attempt an escape plan, my stomach dropped. Stefan's parents were sitting at the kitchen island, casually sipping coffee deep in conversation, blissfully unaware that I had occupied their son's bed last night.

Olivia looked up first. She seemed poised and beautiful, even without the glamorous makeup she's often photographed wearing. Her sharp eyes met mine, and I could see the gears turning as she tried to recall where she knew me from. *You won't, lady, but please don't ask.*

"Good morning," she said. "I don't think we've met before."

I forced a smile that likely resembled a grimace. "Uh, good morning. I'm Abby. I'm… a friend of Stefan's," I lied.

The air in the room thickened with tension, reminiscent of Bangkok's notorious smog-choked skies during the burning season.

My voice trembled despite my efforts to sound composed, and I could sense her skepticism. *Great, she doesn't believe me. Not that I blame her.*

Olivia's smile remained polite, though it had taken on a distant edge.

"It's nice to meet you," she said. "Stefan hasn't mentioned you before."

I found myself beyond caring. My sole focus narrowed to a desperate desire: escape. My need to flee was urgent and primal.

"Oh, we-uh-we just met recently," I stammered.

"I should probably leave; I don't want to take up any more of your time."

Robert barely looked up from his coffee, which I took as my cue to escape. Without awaiting a response, I turned toward the door as my heart pounded. The cool air hit me as soon as I stepped outside, bringing a rush of relief—but it didn't erase the sinking feeling in my stomach. *Great, they probably think I'm just another of his many girlfriends.* I shook my head and sighed.

### Stefan

Her faint scent lingered on my sheets—soft and sweet, like her lips. My sluggish mind struggled to recognize that I was alone in bed, the space beside me empty.

Yawning, memories began to flood back—Abby. The quiet, bookish girl who entered my life on a dare. She was nothing like the women I typically surrounded myself with: no practiced seduction, no air of calculated confidence. An innocence about her was impossible to ignore, as if she didn't even realize the effect she had.

When I kissed her, the softness of her skin and her big, surprised doe eyes captivated me. Abby wasn't merely different; she was unforgettable. That realization struck me more than I cared to admit.

Why had I let myself cross that line? I brought her home. That was a first. None of my usual bed buddies ever made it past the front door, let alone into my bed.

Typically, my encounters occurred in my dorm room and were strictly no-frills—no kissing, no lovemaking, nothing that could be mistaken for intimacy, nothing too personal, messy, or likely to come with strings. I didn't like entanglement. I preferred to keep things simple: fun without complications, passion without permanence.

But with her, it felt different. When our lips met, I couldn't help but savor her soft, plump lips. The sounds escaped her throat like caffeine to my ears; I couldn't just take a sip; I had to drink the whole cup. I was surprised by how much I enjoyed kissing her. My hand reached out, seeking her warmth beside me, only to find cold, empty sheets. She wasn't there. I looked at the bed and nightstand to see if she had left a note or anything behind. I was left with nothing but disappointment and the remnants of her presence.

How had she slipped past all those rules?

I sat up, kicked the sheets off my legs, and glanced at the clock: 9:30 AM. She must have slipped out while I was asleep—again. This was the second time she had pulled off a disappearing act, which bothered me for some reason.

It wasn't that I had any reason to feel this way. Still, the thought of her sneaking off left an uncomfortable knot in my chest. *Why do I care?* I needed to get a grip fast. It was too early on a Saturday for me to pretend to be functional, let alone spiral over Abby.

What good would it do to lie here thinking about her? Since I was already awake, I might as well act like it. Reluctantly, I swung my legs over the side of the bed, stood up, put on a t-shirt, and headed downstairs, hoping some coffee would help jumpstart my day.

When I entered the kitchen, I didn't expect the tension that awaited me. Mom sat at the breakfast table, cradling her coffee. Dad stood behind the counter; his brow furrowed so deeply that it seemed he was in a crisis. They both looked up as I came in, and I knew I was facing another lecture.

"Stefan," Mom began, "we need to talk.

"You know exactly what," Dad interjected. He set his cup down with a clink and gave the Dad Stare—the look that made him seem ten feet tall, even though I was taller.

"This behavior, Stefan," he continued, his words slow and measured as if he were about to deliver a verdict in court. "The parties and the endless stream of meaningless hookups—it must stop."

Ah, there it was: the intervention from the disappointed parents. It was classic Saturday morning entertainment.

I leaned against the counter and took another sip of my caffeine fix to buy myself a little more time.

"There's nothing to discuss," I said, my tone sharper than I had intended. "You don't need to worry about my relationships; they're my business, not yours."

Dad shot me a look. "It's not just the relationships, Stefan. It's the fact that you don't seem to care about anything real. You need to start taking things more seriously—"

"I'm serious," I interrupted, setting my mug down more forcefully than necessary. "About my own life. So, can we please drop it?" I suspect they must have seen Abby when she left. One reason I don't bring girls home is to avoid this very situation. "You don't even know who she is, so there's no need to make this a bigger deal than it is."

They exchanged one of those loaded parental glances. "All we're saying," Mom began, is that you should find a good young woman to date and build a meaningful relationship with." "Because at this rate," she continued, "it's only a matter of time before someone shows up pregnant."

"Just... think about it," Dad says.

I plastered on a tight smile. "Sure, I'll consider what you said." With that, I walked out of the kitchen, but not before catching Dad's comment. "He better listen; otherwise, he'll have countless regrets he can't undo."

The words lingered, but I brushed them off with practiced ease. *Whatever.* They didn't understand—they never had.

I picked up my keys from the counter and tried not to dwell on their words or the heavy sensation in my chest. Abby was gone, and whatever last night had been—whatever part of me had wished it could be—didn't matter now.

# Chapter Seven

## Abby

It was a Wednesday afternoon, and I was trying, for the millionth time, to focus on the lecture in front of me. While my professor, an older man, droned on about the origins of literary theory, modernism, or something along those lines, I felt my attention drifting. Honestly, I had stopped paying attention about ten minutes ago, and his words were like background noise. This was so unlike me. My mind kept returning to Stefan for some reason. It was just a silly crush, I told myself. But who was I kidding?

A sudden ping from my phone drew my attention back to the present. I felt a nervous flutter in my stomach when I noticed the Socialtiez notification in the corner of my screen.

Stefan Jackson is now following you.

My breath caught in my throat. What on earth is happening?

I knew he followed pretty much everyone in school. I wasn't naive enough to think his following meant anything special, but I still felt warm and giddy.

I stared at the notification, uncertain about what to do. My fingers twitched against the screen. Then, on a whim, I clicked on his profile. His feed was just as I expected, pictures of him looking effortlessly handsome, whether at a sports game, standing in front of a ridiculous luxury car, or at an event with his parents. Each photo had thousands of likes and comments, some flirty, others filled with praise.

Curiosity got the better of me."

And before I knew it, I was scrolling through his profile page like a detective assembling clues. Picture after picture, my heart leapt for reasons I couldn't quite articulate—was it intrigue? Nervousness? Or something far worse, like interest?

Minutes ticked by as I hovered over the 'Follow Back' button, debating whether this was a good or bad idea. But before I could overthink myself into oblivion, I pressed it.

My phone vibrated almost instantly in my hand. Well, that didn't take long at all.

**Stefan Jackson:**

"Hey, McKenna. You missed me, didn't you? So eager to follow me."

I nearly choked on my saliva. His playful message caught me entirely off guard. A grin spread across my face before I could stop, making me feel like a fool. I glanced around the lecture hall, my eyes darting nervously over my classmates' faces, even though I knew none of them had a clue who I was texting—or why my heart was suddenly making crazy moves.

**Me:**

"Don't flatter yourself; I just happen to be online."

I could see the smirk in his response.

**Stefan:**

"McKenna, online? In class? Is the world coming to an end?"

I bit my lip. As my heart skipped with an excitement I wasn't accustomed to, I realized I had never experienced this kind of playful back-and-forth before.

Well, perhaps with Jack, my best friend, but that was different. Jack never made my pulse race or my cheeks flush like this. With him, it's platonic.

**Me:**

"Maybe I'm going through my rebellious phase."

**Stefan:**

"Would you mind including me in the fun?"

My cheeks flushed, and my heart fluttered at his words. It was silly, but there was something about how he made everything sound so tempting and effortless. I was definitely in over my head here. Yet, it wasn't as if I didn't enjoy the attention. It felt nice to be desired.

The conversation flowed easily afterward, with Stefan teasing me and me responding with my playful retorts.

It didn't take long for the class to end, and I shoved my phone back into my bag, still buzzing with the energy of our conversation.

As I entered the hall, I stood in stunned silence.

Stefan was leaning casually against a wall near the exit. His usual swagger was evident, his curly brown hair slightly tousled by the wind, and his eyes scanned his phone. Next to him stood his friends—Mason, Kevin, and the others I had seen at the party.

I turned around quickly, pretending I didn't see them, but luck wasn't on my side. The clearing of a throat echoed, followed by, "Well, if it isn't Miss McKenna." I slowly turned back and was met with a cunning grin. He pushed off the wall and stepped into my path. I suddenly felt stares at me at his greeting. I was sure they were curious about what happened that night, but I tried to ignore them all; my ears reddened with awareness. "I didn't expect to see you out here all by yourself. I guess people do change after all."

I rolled my eyes, stifling a smile. "And I see you never change."

"Ooh, sick burn," Mason says, and Stefan raises his hands in surrender, flashing a brilliant grin. "I'm looking for someone to change me if you understand." He wiggles his eyebrows at me suggestively.

"Hey, she doesn't need someone like you," Kevin chimed in, nudging Mason's shoulder with a grin. "We all know she could do better."

My cheeks felt hot at the sudden attention, but I played it off. I shot them a playful glare and joined in on their banter. Chuckling, I said, "I sure can."

They laughed loudly, but not at me. It felt as though we were friends. There was warmth in their teasing, so I knew they didn't mean anything by it.

It's hard to believe that these guys and I barely crossed paths just a few weeks ago. Stefan and I had sociology class together, and we were partners at one point. I had a passing fancy for him during my first and second years, but I quickly got over it because guys can't be trusted, and I wasn't even his type.

47

"Aw, come on, McKenna," Stefan said with a wink as he relished in the moment. "You could use a bit of fun in your life."

I glanced at him, narrowing my eyes. "No thanks, Stefan. I'll find other ways to have fun." With that, I turned on my heels and walked away, a smile as gigantic as the sun lighting up my face. I was fully aware of the lighthearted teasing still echoing behind me.

# Chapter Eight

## Abby

It had been five days since I last saw Stefan- five days of sporadic messages I re-read like some lovesick teenager. It wasn't supposed to be like this. I wasn't meant to sit around with my phone in hand, waiting for his next message to pop up. But here I was. Who am I? Over the years, I prided myself on my studies and strict schedule, and now...I was hanging on every word Stefan Jackson sent my way.

I felt a thrill each time his name lit up my screen. Even his most casual messages made my heart skip a beat.

### Stefan:

"I'm still waiting for you to prove you can let loose a bit."

I hadn't responded to that one yet. Every time I attempt to type, my fingers linger over the keyboard, trying to figure out how to reply without sounding desperate. Was it too soon to admit I liked how he flirted with me? The idea of stepping outside my comfort zone with him was appealing. He was just so easygoing and fun. Everything felt so natural with him.

Before the dare, I didn't engage in spontaneous, wild activities because I preferred structure and enjoyed knowing precisely what would happen next. However, something about Stefan made the unknown feel less intimidating.

The ping of yet another text message startled me. I glanced at the screen.

**Stefan:**

"Are you available? Would you like to meet up this evening?"

His simple question sent me into a frenzy. "Meet him tonight? Like a date?" "Was it a date? No, it couldn't be. Could it? Of course not." This was the first time Stefan had ever asked to hang out.

My eyes flicked to the clock—5:30 PM.

**Me:**

"What time were you thinking?"

**Stefan:**

"7:00 PM or 8:00 PM."

"Ugh! Do I have enough time to figure this out? Was I planning to do this?"

**Me:** 8:00 PM works for me.

I glanced up from my phone at my roommates, who were also in the living room. Alexis lay on the couch, browsing through her phone, while Jess flipped through her textbook. I reopened my phone to confirm that I had read his message correctly.

"What's behind that smile?" Alexis asked.

"What smile?" I replied, quickly closing my phone and pretending to be nonchalant.

"Abby," Alexis said, squinting at me.

"Don't play coy," Jess said. "You've been mysterious all afternoon."

"What do you mean? You all are weird. I'm just...studying."

"Sure," Alexis drawled. "Studying... or texting a certain someone?"

"Nope! I—I was reading an email."

"Uh-huh, an email," Alexis said sarcastically. "And I suppose that email is from... Stefan?"

I tense up; indeed, I'm too predictable.

"Well?" Jessica urged. "You're not fooling anyone. Come on, spill."

My face got hot. "I'm just—just talking to him. It's no big deal," I lied. "You guys are way too nosy. "I jumped to my feet to escape. "I'll see you later."

"Wait," Alexis says, a spark of playfulness in her eyes. "Are you going out tonight? You're meeting him, right?"

I looked around and asked, "Who?" feigning ignorance about whom she was referring to.

"Abby," Alexis laughed, shaking her head. "You've got that look in your eyes. Please stop trying to hide it. You're going on a date with Stefan."

I swallowed, feeling my pulse quicken. "It's not a date," I protested weakly. "I don't know; we're just hanging out."

Jessica perked up, clearly excited by the idea. "Come on, Abbs! You've got to tell us everything now."

And that's how I gave in and shared everything that led to today's text. "Now he wants to meet up. I'm not even sure if it's a date or not." "Maybe it's just dinner."

"Dinner with Stefan Jackson, huh? Sure, Abby," Alexis replied. Jessica shot her a knowing glance.

"We'll be here eagerly awaiting all the juicy details."

I shook my head.

"Do you need help finding an outfit for your date?" they asked with a smile.

"You two are insufferable."

"Oh yes, Alexis, when I get back, I want to know what happened between you and Kevin the night we went clubbing." Her expression changed suddenly. With that, I hurried upstairs.

My excitement and nerves were overwhelming. I didn't know what to expect from tonight. It could be awkward, or even a disaster. But then again, it could also be... pleasant.

On the ride to the restaurant, I felt like a nervous wreck. Everything about this felt a bit reckless yet also exhilarating. The restaurant wasn't far from town but tucked away from the main street and other eateries. It featured a cozy, intimate atmosphere, with warm lights glowing through the windows and several cars parked outside.

When I walked in, no one was at the front desk, so I took it upon myself to look around. My stomach fluttered again when I spotted him. Stefan was sitting at a booth near the back. He looked handsome, as always. His sharp cheekbones and confident demeanor made him resemble someone who belonged on a magazine cover.

"Hi, how many are in your party?" A lady asked as she approached the front desk. I pointed to him. He glanced up right then, and his face lit up with that signature smile that made my heart flutter annoyingly.

"McKenna," he said as I sat down.

"You came."

"Of course I did," I responded with a smile.

I slid into the booth across from him, ignoring my trembling hands. "You didn't think I'd back out, did you?"

"I never know what to expect from you," he shrugged, his eyes sparkling with amusement.

"I am a woman of my word."

"I'm glad you're here," he says.

A waiter approached, and we ordered drinks and food—nothing too fancy, just a burger, fries, and lasagna. It was enough to make ourselves comfortable. I couldn't help but feel a bit awkward, though. We were alone. No crowds. No loud music. Just country music playing in the background, and the two of us sitting across from each other in the quiet, dimly lit diner.

"Do you usually hang out here?" I inquired, glancing around at the rustic and charming decor. The diner felt as if it had been here for decades, tucked away from the hustle and bustle of the city.

"Not always, but I enjoy the peace," Stefan said with a wink. "Sometimes, it's nice to have a moment to yourself. You know?" Plus, I thought you'd appreciate it here." Also, the food is delicious.

I nodded, feeling a warm sensation. It made me feel special, as if I was getting a glimpse of another side of him—the side he didn't reveal to anyone else. And I didn't know what to make of that.

We spent the rest of the evening getting to know each other, even touching on our plans after graduation. I found out that he wants to become a football coach. This was an unexpected surprise, as I had thought he was going into business.

# Chapter Nine

## Abby

The next day, I woke up feeling good. The butterflies in my chest felt unfamiliar and fresh. Just the thought of him gave me a rush, like a dose of dopamine. It was intoxicating!

I spent the morning preparing for class, putting a little extra care into my outfit—a cozy cardigan and comfortable yet flattering jeans. My hair, usually pulled back into a simple ponytail, was down today, with loose waves framing my face. For the first time in a while, I felt good about myself—confident, even.

I grabbed a protein shake and a banana as we prepared for the day. Then, I headed off with Alexis and Jessica toward campus.

"Cute outfit!" Jessica complimented.

"Thank you," I replied.

"Our girl is looking good for her soon-to-be boyfriend," Alexis joked.

A wishful smile spread across my face, and I playfully pushed them as we walked. The cool morning breeze accompanied us.

Just another typical day at university, I'm in my Pedagogy and Teaching class, focused on jotting down notes on curriculum development and assessment techniques. I also participated when necessary. Yet, Stefan had temporarily taken residence in my brain. I think I was falling for him. He made me want to let go of all the rules I'd been following.

After class, I decided to visit the campus coffee shop, humming a tune softly to myself. I ordered a vanilla bean Frappuccino and a slice of coffee cake. I stepped out of the coffee shop and headed toward the quad with my treats. But what I saw felt like a sucker punch to my abdomen.

Stefan sat on one of the benches, his arm around a girl— Lisa, I believe that was her name. She leaned into him, her hand resting on his chest. My stomach twisted uncomfortably; the butterflies that once felt so sweet were now turning sour.

I don't know what possessed me, but I walked over to them, my legs moving before my brain could catch up. I had to talk to him; I needed to understand why.

I stood before them, my heart pounding. "Stefan, can we talk for a minute?"

Lisa's eyes flicked to me, her smile swiftly transforming into disdain. She tilted her pretty blonde head, clearly unhappy about the interruption. "Uh, excuse me, but we're on a date here. Are you blind?"

I felt a heat rising in my chest; the old Abby, who avoided conflict, vanished momentarily. "I don't care," I snapped. "I need to talk to Stefan."

Stefan's gaze flicked my way, and for a moment, I thought I detected a flicker of guilt in his eyes. Yet, I dismissed it like everything else. He stood up, his expression hardening. Without saying a word to Lisa, he followed me.

"What is it, Abby?"

I couldn't stop myself from asking him a question. "Why did you take me on a date last night if you were going to do this? It hasn't even been 24 hours yet?"

He let out a frustrated sigh. "Look, Abby, I don't know what you think this is, but we aren't dating. We went out last night because it was fun. You're reading too much into it."

His words struck me like a slap. I blinked and stepped back, trying to regain my composure. Was that all I had been to him? Just fun? Did he think I was just another girl, a casual fling to add to his list?

"Fun?" "That's all this was? You didn't even have the decency to explain before I caught you with someone else?"

Stefan glanced at me briefly and sighed again. "Abby, I don't owe you anything. Last night was... enjoyable, but it doesn't equate to any unspoken commitment. You need to adjust your expectations."

I stood frozen, stunned, as I struggled to comprehend his brutal dismissal.

To make matters worse, I heard a chuckle and turned to see Lisa and her friends laughing.

The embarrassment and hurt were unbearable; I could feel the tears welling at the corners of my eyes.

True, we hadn't defined our connection with labels or promises. Our relationship existed in that hazy space between casual and significant. At least, that's what I believed. I never anticipated such a harsh rejection. It felt as though Stefan had siphoned and extinguished the warmth from our shared moments.

"Was this the reason you brought me there?" I whispered. "Because you didn't want to be seen with me?"

He appeared shocked by my question. "Don't be ridiculous, I—"

I no longer trusted myself to speak. I turned on my heel and walked away.

I barely made it home. The walk back from campus felt endless, each step heavy as if I were trudging through wet concrete. My heart felt like it was being squeezed from every direction, a pressure so tight that I feared I might not be able to breathe. I wanted to scream and question why I think it could be different? Why did I believe that someone like Stefan Jackson would care about me?

When I reached our apartment, I slammed the door behind me as if the world outside had no power to hurt me anymore. I tossed my bag aside and stumbled to my room, dropping face-first onto my bed, my body feeling like it was made of lead. The tears that had been threatening all day finally came, but they didn't come easily. I fought them at first, stubbornly pressing my face into the pillow, trying to hide the ugly sobs that escaped from my throat. It felt so hard to breathe.

"Why does this hurt so much? "I asked myself, but nothing made sense. I hadn't even dated Stefan. We'd spent a couple of nights together, and I foolishly thought it meant more than it did. I got caught up in how he looked at me and how he made me feel like I mattered. I became attached, even though I knew better.

# Chapter Ten

# Abby

The door creaked as it slowly opened. A few minutes later, I heard the soft shuffle of footsteps entering the room. I didn't have to look up to know it was Alexis and Jessica.

"Abby?" Alexis says softly, as if she sensed something was wrong. "What's the matter?"

I didn't answer. I couldn't. The lump in my throat was too large to swallow, so I just lay there, my face still buried in the pillow.

"Abbs, honey, what's wrong? What happened?" Jessica inquired.

When I finally lifted my head, I felt like a bobblehead. It was so heavy that I thought I would topple over. My eyes were swollen, and my face was flushed. I wiped my cheeks, but it was in vain. The tears kept flowing.

"I…I feel so... foolish. Stefan embarrassed me in front of Lisa, saying that our relationship was fun but nothing more." I don't understand why I'm so upset." "I mean, he's right, we weren't even in a relationship."

Alexis sat beside me on the bed, her usual brash demeanor much softer. Jess climbed onto the bed and wrapped me in a tight hug.

"You're not foolish," Alexis said, surprising me by joining the hug. "You have feelings for him. You allowed yourself to be vulnerable, and that's okay. It's normal to feel this way."

I let out a shaky breath, unable to hold back another sob that turned into hiccups.

"But it doesn't make sense. Why am I acting this way? Why does it hurt so much? It was only a few weeks. I should be fine." "It's not like we've been together for years."

"Hey, these things rarely make sense," Jess said, holding me tighter. "You connected with him, Abbs. You let your guard down. Emotions aren't logical; they don't follow rules. It's okay to feel heartbroken, even if you weren't officially together. Just give it some time; it'll hurt less," she reassured me.

That was it—the realization I had been avoiding. I had opened up to him in a way that was uncharacteristic of me. I felt something I've never felt before. I gave him my body, hoping that maybe, just maybe, someone like Stefan would truly understand me. After my father left and my mom was hurt, I had lost hope of ever opening my heart to anyone. Instead, I focused on my studies. This way, the only person who could disappoint me was myself. However, as time passed and we got to know each other better, I let go of my rules and allowed myself to experience love.

"I thought… I thought maybe we could be more," I choked out. "I believed he cared. He made me feel special, as if I were the only one. Now I see him with her, and I feel foolish. Like I was just a momentary pleasure."

"You're not," Alexis said. "You're right; he doesn't get to toy with your emotions like that, making you feel something genuine and then move on as if it meant nothing."

"I knew it was casual. I knew it. But I still... I still let myself believe. Why is it so hard to let go?" I asked, frustrated.

"Because you're human, Abbs," Jessica replied softly. "Just take it easy on yourself."

"Thanks," I said appreciatively.

I cried again, not only for Stefan and his words but also for myself, for my unrequited love and unrealistic expectations.

"I just wanted to be seen." Is that too much to ask? "I wanted someone to recognize and love me for who I am."

"We see you, Abby, and we love you," Alexis said. "We've always seen you. You're amazing. No guy, no matter how attractive or charming, gets to make you feel less than you are. You deserve someone who sees and loves you just as deeply as you love them."

### Stefan

I sat on the couch in my dorm room, staring at my phone. I didn't register what Kevin and Mason were saying, but I could guess that they were probably talking about which party we would crash this weekend, and Mason was most likely discussing who he would hook up with. My attention, however, was elsewhere.

I felt terrible about what I said to her. The hurt in her eyes before she left that day ate at me.

"Damn, why was I such a jerk?" I couldn't shake the guilt.

A week had passed since the incident, but time didn't make me feel better. Instead, I couldn't stop replaying the event like a song stuck in my head. The way her voice trembled before she left—I could still hear the echo of her footsteps as she moved further away from me.

My friends' voices grew louder, bringing me back to the present moment.

"Yo, Stefan!" Mason called out suddenly, snapping me out of my daze.

"Are you okay, man?"

"Yeah, I'm just tired," I replied.

"Come on, man," he said. "You've been 'tired' for a week now. What's going on with you?"

"Yeah, dude, you've been on some weird shit lately, always lost in your thoughts," Kevin added.

"Honestly, I did something awful."

"You got someone knocked up?" Mason asked.

"No fool, why would you even say that?"

"What did you do then?" Kevin questioned.

"Something dumb; I can't explain it." How could I articulate how much I hated myself right now? The person I was that day- I detested that version of myself.

"Is it your parents' or ladies' trouble?" Mason teased, glancing at me. "You've been sulking around like a lovesick puppy."

I opened my mouth to deny it, but what was the point of lying? They knew me well enough. I let out a frustrated sigh.

"It's a girl problem."

Their heads shot up as if my words were the cranks of a jack-in-the-box toy; only the sound was broken as the room fell silent.

"Wait, what?" Mason asked, "You? Of all people, have girl problems?"

"Yes," I replied.

"Damn, we're all doomed then, "Kevin said.

"I messed up."

Mason's interest was apparent as his eyes widened, and he moved closer. "Messed up? How? What did you do?"

"I said and did many stupid things," I replied. "And I... I hurt her. I didn't mean to, but I did."

"Whoa. You? Hurt someone? Since when do you care? "Kevin asked, intrigued as well. "I've never seen you like this before. Who is she?"

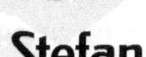

# Chapter Eleven

## Stefan

I racked my brain about what to say. I couldn't honestly claim to like her. I was ashamed; scratch that, I'm appalled at myself. But I needed their help to devise a plan. "It's Abby." Saying her name and recalling how things had ended made my stomach churn.

"I had been talking to her a lot lately, and we had gone on a date at the diner, where we had a good time. However, my dad and I had another argument that morning, which upset me...

"Go on," Kevin says.

The room was quiet once more as they awaited my explanation.

This time, it wasn't the usual Stefan-style explanation.

"Lisa and I have been having fun off and on for a while. "You know how it is." "So, when she asked to go out, it felt like something I was supposed to do. I didn't even think twice about it. And I mean, Abby and I aren't dating, so I didn't see anything wrong with it."

Abby saw us and confronted me about it while I was still fuming from my earlier encounter. I told her we weren't in a relationship, so I didn't owe her any explanation. She looked so hurt when she left."

They were silent in the wake of my rant. "Abby? As in Abby McKenna? Mason asked.

I nodded. "Yes, that's the only Abby McKenna we both know."

I sat up straight, hoping my negative thoughts would stop.

"I need your help developing a plan to get her back.

Mason looked shocked. "Dude, what's wrong with you?" "I knew you had a thing for her since the freshman. I was surprised to see her at the party because she rarely attends these events. That's why I took a shot for you by daring her to sleep with you. I figured you would still be on her mind even if she declined the dare and decided to drink."

"When did I tell you I liked her?"

"You didn't say it outright, but during freshman year, you kept talking about how nice she was when she lent you her charger. You even said she smelled good.

"Look, correct me if I'm wrong," Kevin said. "I think you're starting to develop feelings for her, so to avoid confronting those feelings, you chose to act like a jerk."

"Maybe," I responded.

"What are you going to do about it?" Mason asks.

I lounged back on the couch. "I don't know; that's why I need your help. She blocked and unfollowed me on Socialtiez and won't even spare me a glance when I see her.

"Thinking about it now, I don't think I would care much if Lisa reacted that way." "However, Abby, she's different. I fidgeted in my seat.

"I want things to go back to normal." "Maybe Dad was right after all.

I didn't want to admit it, but the truth was that Abby had completely thrown me off track. She had snuck far beyond my epidermis and reached the mediastinum, a place no other woman had reached except for my mom and grandma. Conversations with her were pleasant; she understood my corny jokes, and I felt at ease as if she knew me in ways I couldn't explain. Her little giggles were charming, and her big eyes were mesmerizing. Being intimate with her was an experience I longed for, and her luscious lips were so kissable. I would do anything to remove the hurt I caused and for her to forgive me.

"Is it strange that I can't stop thinking about her?"

"Nope, she makes you feel something special," Mason says.

There was no need to argue because he wasn't wrong. I wasn't accustomed to feeling anything for anyone other than the occasional fling. My past relationships didn't require much. But when it came to Abby, she's incredible, and I would love to give us a chance if she gives me the opportunity.

"I don't know what I should do. I know I'm not good enough for her. What if I mess it up again?" I don't want to hurt her anymore.

"Dude, from what I heard, you've already ruined it," Kevin replied.

I winced; the thought of her avoiding me as if I were some toxic person, though I deserved it, didn't sit right with me.

"Then you need to apologize," Kevin said. "Be sincere, help her understand how truly sorry you are, and assure her that it won't happen again."

"I don't know if I can mend what I did, but I plan to try."

"It won't be easy," Mason says. On some serious shit, I think you're in love with her. Don't pretend you're not. It's evident to anyone around you these past few weeks."

I scoffed, instantly dismissing the idea. "That's absurd. I'm not—"

"Yeah, you are," Kevin cut me off. "You're just too scared to admit it. But it's obvious to us." "You've been a mess because of her, and here we are having this conversation instead of our usual ones, and you can't figure out what to do with yourself. That's love, man. When someone shakes you up like this and leaves you feeling like you're spinning in circles."

I stared at him, stunned. Love? I hadn't allowed myself to think of it that way. Hell, I didn't even want to. The concept of love made everything seem heavy and complicated, and I wasn't ready. Not when everything felt so uncertain. But deep down, a part of me couldn't deny what they were saying. Abby had changed something inside me. And I don't know if that was a good thing or a bad thing.

Of course, you would know you've only been in love with Alexis for like ever. And where has that gotten you? I wanted to say, but I decided against it. I had my own shit to worry about.

"Look, we are just going in circles. Here's what you should do: stop moping around and fight for her. Go to her and do everything you can to show her how much she means to you. Because right now, you're very close to losing her for good. And if you're okay with that, fine. But I don't think you are," Kevin said.

They were right. I had no more excuses. If I want Abby back, I have to be willing to go all in—no more running, no more pretending. There was no doubt in my mind.

"Alright," I said, standing up and shaking off any lingering doubts. "I'll resolve this."

"That's right, GO GET YOUR GIRL! "Mason shouted, both he and Kevin smiling.

# Chapter Twelve

## Abby

It has been a month, four excruciating weeks since everything fell apart. And yet, here I am—still trapped in the aftermath of it all. Stefan tried to contact me, but I blocked him. I also unfollowed him on Socialtiez. He's attempted to talk to me around campus, but I've given him the cold shoulder. Trying to get over him has been difficult because I see him everywhere. I feel suffocated. As a logical person with keen observation, I believe I can see through the bullshit. But Stefan—damn him—he broke through every wall I'd built around myself. I let him in. And now look at me.

I couldn't even explain why I let it get this far. How did I allow a dare to turn my simple, comfortable life upside down? I knew exactly what he was: a playboy. A man with a reputation for never sticking around, who flirted with every girl in sight and probably slept with half of them. I might be judging, but he never made any real effort to hide it. Yet somewhere along the way, I convinced myself that I was different, that somehow, I could be the one for him, or at the very least, the one he would treat differently.

I knew better. I should have known better. I felt restless walking across campus, terrified of seeing him again.

Before I even heard footsteps, a tug on my arm caught my attention. A hand gripped my wrist, yanking me to the side. My body reacted instinctively; I recoiled, pulling away and trying to break free from whoever it was. My body recognized his touch before I came face-to-face with him.

My pulse spiked, and I could feel the rage that had been building inside me surfacing— anger I had worked so hard to suppress over the past few days.

I pulled back, my eyes narrowed, and my lips curled into a sneer. "What the hell do you want?"

"McKenna, wait." He said my name as if we were close, like it meant something. "I need to talk to you. Please, "he urged.

The sight of him made me furious. My heart pounded in my chest, and my stomach churned. "Talk," I scoffed incredulously. "After everything? You humiliated me, Stefan. You made me feel like the dirt beneath your feet, and now you say you want to talk?" "Well, I'm not interested in what you have to say."

I tried to step back again, but he was persistent, moving with me, his hand gripping my arm, pulling me toward him. I jerked away. "Don't touch me!" I took a deep breath and added, "You were right, so I took your advice and adjusted my expectations. We are nothing to each other, so please leave me alone."

"I was wrong; please give me a chance to apologize and make it up to you," he pleaded.

I stepped back again, shaking my head at him. "No. No, I don't want to talk to you. After what you did? Are you serious?"

"I'm a jerk, I know. I—" He continued to reach for me, attempting to get closer, but I didn't want him near me. Every inch he moved toward me deepened the pit in my stomach, and I was on the verge of a full-blown panic attack.

"Abby, please hear me out," he begged, almost desperately.

"A jerk? A jerky, you say?" I couldn't hold it in any longer and snapped. The words tumbled out quickly and forcefully, as everything poured out. "A jerk is too nice of a word. Do you have any idea how much I trusted you? How much I believe in you? I genuinely thought you might be different, that maybe you'd care about me, even just a little. But no. You don't care about anyone but yourself, Stefan."

Sorrow was evident in his eyes, yet I could no longer trust it.

I took another step back, and then I felt it—tears. Hot, burning tears stung my eyes before falling and slipping down my cheeks, and I didn't even try to stop them. I was so furious. So hurt. So... broken. All this pain, all these emotions that I thought I had under control, came rushing out, and I couldn't stop it.

I clutched my chest as I gasped for air. This is not who I am. I never fall apart like this. But I couldn't stop. I couldn't even breathe.

I didn't know how long I stood there, sobbing and gasping for air; it felt like an eternity. The rage had consumed me, and all that remained was emptiness.

Stefan stood still, his hands reached out to me, but didn't touch me, as if he was afraid of making things worse. No one other than Mom and Jack has ever seen me like this. I never allow anyone to witness my breaking point. But this? This was entirely on him. This happened because of him.

"I can't do this," I choked out between sobs. "You've —" I stopped, wiping my eyes with the back of my hand to regain control, but I couldn't. It's too much. "I've never felt like this before. I don't know what to do with all of this—this mess inside me now. And it's because of you. It's because of what you did. I can't just... pretend it didn't happen."

Stefan took a hesitant step forward. He stared at me, looking utterly lost, and for the first time, I noticed it— genuine regret. I almost wish I hadn't because it only made this harder.

"I'm so sorry, Abby," he said gently. "I never wanted to hurt you. I never meant for it to go this far...it wasn't supposed to be like this."

"Then why did you?" I demanded, though it was more a hiccup than a question. "Why did you let me believe you cared? Why did you make me think... think that I matter to you?"

I turned and left him speechless as I walked far away from him. He doesn't stop me this time.

I don't know what I want from him. I don't know if I could ever forgive him. But right now, I need time alone because I will only keep falling if I don't. And I've had enough of that.

# Chapter Thirteen

## Abby

My adrenaline still had me buzzing as if it were prep week, and I was high on Red Bull. My thoughts were scattered pieces of a puzzle I couldn't assemble.

I walked into my room, ignoring the concerned looks from Alexis and Jessica on the couch. They didn't understand. They didn't live in my head, where everything suddenly fell apart. The dare. Stefan. The way he looked at me made me feel—so... unlike myself. I hated it with all my being.

I needed to get away and clear my mind. I began shoving clothes into my backpack, mindlessly grabbing whatever I could find: a hoodie, jeans, and a couple of shirts. It didn't matter. My hands moved frantically, and I barely registered the mess I was creating. The room felt too small and suffocating.

"Abbs," Jess said, slicing through the din of my chaotic packing. "What's going on?"

I was preoccupied with stuffing clothes into the bag while I struggled against the unsettling urge to respond. Alexis was determined to pierce my silence.

"You're not going anywhere, Abby. Don't make a hasty decision. The finals are just a few weeks away. You need to study, not run off to some place to escape... whatever this is."

"I'm just going home for a few days," I said, almost inaudibly.

"Then why are you packing?" Jess asked.

I had no answer for her, so I kept my back turned.

"Home?" she repeated, disbelief dripping from every syllable. "Really? I don't know what just happened, but you can't just let a guy mess with your head like this. Don't let Stefan ruin your life, Abby. You're better than this."

I paused; my hands stilled mid-air as I reached for another shirt. I bit my lower lip to suppress my feelings. "You don't understand," I spat. "You've always just... done whatever you wanted. It's not the same for me. It has never been like that for me. Do you think I wanted this? To be stuck in this mess?"

Alexis's eyes flashed with hurt as she uncrossed her arms and moved closer to me. "No one's saying you asked for anything, Abby. But this isn't the way to deal with it. You're acting like a scared little girl, running home simply because you fear facing the situation. You can't just give up every time things get uncomfortable. What about your future? What about your studies? What about us?"

Her words stung. I was angry—so angry. I was angry at myself for getting caught up in Stefan's world, enraged at the whole situation, and infuriated at how quickly everything escalated when I never even wanted it to begin.

"I'm not you, Alexis!" "I can't be reckless and carefree. I have responsibilities. I need to be responsible. I need to escape from this. And you—" I paused, realizing I was about to say something I might regret. Yet, the words spilled out anyway. "You're the reason I even did this. You two are the reason I'm caught up in all this now. You pushed me to take risks when all I've ever wanted was to stay safe."

Alexis's face was indifferent. "That's not fair, Abby. You can't blame us for your choices. We were only trying to help you see that there's more to life than sticking to the same damn routine all the time. And this"—she gestured to my packed backpack—" is you running away from it all. You're acting like you can't handle anything."

My hands clenched into fists at my sides, my knuckles white. The tension in the room was high. I felt utterly lost. I didn't know if I was more upset at Stefan, Alexis, Jessica, and the entire world, or myself.

"Maybe I can't handle it," I hissed. "Maybe I'm tired of trying to manage everything all the time. I'm exhausted."

My words hung between us. Alexis was about to say something, but Jess, who had been silent this whole time, spoke up.

"Okay, okay," she said like a parent stopping their children from fighting. "Let's all take a breather. Abby, I understand why you want to leave. I do. But you're not thinking right now. You're just angry, and I get that. However, running home won't solve it. If you want space, we'll stay out of your way. You don't have to return home.

My chest tightened and my throat burned as I held back tears. I didn't want to cry in front of them again, but I was so tired.

"Why does everyone always think they know what's best for me?"

"I don't know what's best for you," says Jess. "But I know you are not the only one going through a tough time. We are your friends, and we want to help you. "Don't shut us out."

There was a lump in my throat, and for a second, I almost gave in. I wanted to scream at them, tell them they didn't understand, and that no one could understand my feelings. But instead, I stood still, then turned away, my mind made up. I couldn't stay here—not in this room or on campus.

I grabbed my backpack and headed for the door. "Let her go, Alexis called after Jess; I didn't stop.

When I flagged down a cab, I didn't care about the money—I didn't care about anything anymore. I just needed to leave.

The cab took me to the bus station, and after what felt like hours, I was on a bus heading home. My phone rang and buzzed a couple of times in my pocket. But I didn't answer. Instead, I silenced it.

Stepped off the bus and headed to our cozy, tiny home. It may not be the largest on the block, but it was the warmest. I felt a sense of relief, even if I knew it was temporary.

# Chapter Fourteen

## Abby

I searched my bag for my keys but couldn't find them. I must have left them in haste. Remembering the spare, I grabbed it from where Mom hid it—tucked under the loose floorboard on the patio—and let myself into the house. The door creaked softly as I pushed it open, and the familiar scent of old wood and fresh air welcomed me back. It had been months since I'd been home. I stepped inside, my sneakers silent against the floor. The house was dim and peaceful in the late evening light.

I bee-lined straight to my room, where everything was neat. The cobalt blue walls and the bookshelf still held all my childhood books. The bed was made just as I left it—crisp and clean, not a wrinkle out of place. I dropped my bag onto the chair by my study desk, kicked off my shoes with a flourish, and flopped onto the bed like a starfish in distress. The mattress was firmer than his—go figure.

Why was I still thinking about him? He was why I came home in the first place, and now he haunted my thoughts. I shook off the mental image and burrowed under my blanket, *which felt cool and heavenly against my skin. I wriggled* around a bit until I found the perfect spot.

I let out a sigh as exhaustion overtook me, and before my mind could spiral into another round of "what-ifs," I was out like a light.

"Abby? What are you doing at home?" Mom asked.

I groaned, blinking into the dim room, trying to focus. There she stood, framed in the doorway—eyes wide, eyebrows practically in orbit as she took in the sight of me.

"I...uh... I came home," I mumbled, my voice still tangled in sleep.

"I see that. Is everything okay?"

She studied me briefly, probably scanning her mental files for any missed texts or calls. "You didn't text or call to say you were coming."

"I didn't want to disturb you at work. Of course, that's only half true, but let's go with it. I thought you were busy," I replied, giving her my best innocent face. She stepped inside my room, her presence comforting. Mom watched me quietly as she analyzed and took stock of my exhausted, rumpled face.

"Abby," she says with concern. "What's going on?" Instantly, my throat tightened, and my eyes threatened to leak. Mom had always been able to draw the truth out of me.

She patted the spot beside her, the universal mom invitation to spill my guts and regress to age six. I didn't hesitate. I buried my face in her shoulder, my body shaking, and my eyes stinging with the urge to cry, even though I was pretty sure my tear ducts were running on fumes at this point.

"It's too much, Mom," I whispered. "Everything feels wrong. I'm supposed to have things figured out. My priorities should be my main focus, not boy problems. I need to be a responsible daughter and make you proud. But lately... I've been doing all the wrong things. I don't even know who I am anymore."

"Honey," she said, threading through my hair, "do I make you feel like you need to be perfect?"

"No."

"So why are you so tough on yourself?"

You've done so much for me that I feel it's only right to be the best daughter for you." However, as graduation approaches, I increasingly feel lost and anxious.

"It's okay to feel lost sometimes. It's also natural to experience heartbreak. No one likes it, but it happens. Remember, you're not supposed to have everything figured out at 21. I still don't have everything figured out, and I'm in my forties."

"I'm just so tired," I choked out. "I've never felt like this before. I don't know what to do."

She didn't respond. Instead, she just held me tighter, rocking me gently like she used to when I was little. We sat there in the hush, the kind that makes you notice the clock's ticking and how your breathing sounds. My eyes still stung, but I felt a little lighter, as if the air in the room had shifted.

"You don't have to do anything right away. Take it easy and don't try to be anyone but yourself," Mom said softly. "Not all change is bad; it's a sign of growing up. Take your time, sweetheart. Let yourself bloom like the flower you are."

I sniffled, rubbing my nose on my sleeve. "But what if I disappoint you?"

She turned my face toward her, her eyes warm.

"Sweetheart, you could never disappoint me. Not ever. Well, unless you drop out of school, become a professional couch potato, and start a cult for lazy people. Then we might need to have a chat."

A sheepish laugh escaped as the knot in my chest loosened a bit. Mom kissed the top of my head and stood, squeezing my shoulder in that way that said, I'm here, even if you don't have the words yet.

"Get some sleep. We'll talk more in the morning— preferably before you join the Potato Club."

I nodded but didn't speak. As I lay back down, I felt her hand on my shoulder.

She didn't ask for explanations or attempt to fix everything. She let me be. And for the first time in days, that was enough.

# Chapter Fifteen

## Abby

As I stepped out of the bathroom, the clatter of dishes and the morning news greeted my ears. The soft shuffle of Mom's flats could be heard from upstairs. It was the kind of everyday comfort that whispered, "Relax. You're home, and everything's fine—for now. School and boy problems can wait." I rolled my neck, wincing at the stiff ache—likely from lying in the same position all night. I don't know if it was because I was home or the prospect of actual breakfast, but the stress from yesterday had vanished, leaving me much calmer.

I tugged on my favorite "vintage" jeans- Mom's old pair that somehow migrated into my closet and never found their way back. I added a slouchy sweatshirt, and voilà, I was ready for the day. Meanwhile, downstairs, Mom was all business. As a medical sales rep, she wore a crisp gray blouse and black slacks, looking ready to close a deal.

The smell of coffee and toast hit me like a wake-up call. Mom was already stationed at the counter, soaking in her daily fix from Nate Blackwood, the anchor she swears is "so reliable"—though we all suspect his thick, lustrous hair won her over. I paused in the doorway, watching her move around the kitchen with ease and efficiency.

She was always so composed, so together—especially after Dad left. Her ability to keep everything running is truly heroic. I stood there, absorbing it all, and thought: if I ever grow up, I hope I'm half as unflappable as she is.

"Morning," I croaked.

Mom glanced up from the toaster, her smile as warm as the kitchen. "Good morning. How's my favorite patient feeling today?"

"Better," I said, though my hair—and probably my face—told a different story.

"That's what I like to hear," she says, sliding a mug of coffee and a plate of food my way. "Eat up, or I'll have to charge you."

"Thanks, Mom."

"You're welcome. Guess who I saw the other day?" She wiggled her eyebrows, clearly expecting me to play along.

My lips pressed tightly as my finger slowly tapped against them, and I spoke. "Let's see… the Queen? Santa? A ghost…"

"You're no fun, she says. It's Jack. I ran into him at the store, and he asked about you."

My heart did a little hop. "Jack? When did he get back?"

A couple of days ago," she replied, buttering her toast.

"That bighead didn't tell me he was back." I couldn't help but smile at the mention of his name.

She paused, knife mid-air, and gave me a look. "Your aunt's over the moon—apparently, he's sticking around for a few weeks. I think she's planning a parade."

I snorted into my coffee. "I'm sure Jack can't wait for the family reunion and the annual 'So, are you two dating yet?' inquisition."

She chuckled. "He's such a good young man. I wish things had worked out between the two of you. But at least you are still friends."

I took a bite of my breakfast and kept eating.

You're probably wondering who Jack is. Well, our relationship is somewhat complicated. We've been friends since our moms swapped pregnancy tips. Legend has it that we fist-bumped in the womb. We did everything together growing up: school projects, summer camps, and a regrettable attempt at a two-person band. It is to be noted that neither of us can sing.

When everyone else was losing their virginity and collecting awkward stories, we thought we would be clever and make each other our "first." I know what you're thinking, but honestly, no regrets. Except, of course, for the part where we tried dating and realized we had more chemistry as lab partners than as lovers.

After high school, Jack went abroad to university, and suddenly our daily routines transformed into time zones and sporadic texts. It wasn't easy, but we stayed in touch for birthdays and the occasional "help, I need advice" emergencies. It's been years since I've seen him in person, but he's never missed sending me a birthday gift—usually something embarrassing enough to make me laugh.

"Have a great day at work, Mom."

"Will do. "Say hi to Jack for me," she yelled. "I love you."

"Love you a bit," I chortled as I grabbed my jacket and headed to Jack's house.

When I stopped before Jack's place, nostalgia washed over me. I walked up to the door, my fist hovering just above the knob. The door swung open before I could even knock. There he was: the man of the hour.

"Abby?" Jack said, stunned. He pulled me into a hug, and I eagerly reciprocated. When we parted, I got a good look at him. He was the same old Jack I knew and loved—the same easy smile and blue eyes. But there was something different about him, too. His hair was shorter, styled to give him a more mature appearance, and his body had filled out. He was broader now—more muscular than I remembered—and my eyes widened slightly at how handsome he had become. Gone was the lanky teenager I used to know. In front of me stood a tall, confident, strong man.

"Wow! Did your head get bigger?" A laugh escaped my lips. "You look... different."

He grins, stepping aside to let me in. "I guess I've been hitting the gym a bit. Looks like your lemons... hit a growth spurt too," he teased.

I shove him playfully, feeling that old sense of comfort you get after slipping on a favorite hoodie.

With Jack, conversation has always been easy, like we'd hit 'pause' instead of 'goodbye.'

"Where's Aunt Jade?" I inquired, glancing around for any sign of her.

"At work," he replied.

"So, what's been going on with you?" Jack asked, leading me to the patio where we had once drawn the blueprints of our future homes with sidewalk chalk.

I took a seat on one of the patio chairs. "You know. College stuff. Classes, roommates, the usual existential crisis—trying to figure out who I am before my student loans do."

"Yeah, I get that. I've been working hard, and I have a few interviews lined up while I'm here, trying to figure out where I'm going next. It's weird to be an adult but still feel like you need adult supervision," he says.

Tell me about it. I'm in the same boat. Except my ship might have a few leaks.

"I was just about to go for a run before your surprise arrival. Do you want to go for a walk instead? he asks.

"Sure," I said with a smile.

As we stroll, we catch up on life, swapping stories and laughing over events that took place when we were young. Despite our time apart, some things about Jack never changed—like his kindness and ability to make me laugh regardless of the situation. And of course, his effortless charisma could charm the socks off anyone. I'm not sure if it's due to our history, but something about being with him feels therapeutic.

"Remember the time you wet the bed thinking you were on the toilet but were asleep?" He says, guffawing.

"Yes, and I also remember when you shit your pants in fourth grade, I cackled.

"It was only a little pebble," he glowered defensively.

I hadn't realized how much I missed this—how much I missed him—until this moment. We had always been each other's rock, even when things became complicated in high school. He was the only guy I could rely on to share my burdens comfortably.

"We have to stay in touch more," I said.

"Yes, especially now that I'll be moving back," he replied. I was over the moon about that.

"I'll be in your area next week; let's meet up," Jack says.

My face lit up in agreement. "Absolutely! Let's do it."

But of course, nothing good lasts forever, as standing at the entrance to the park was a sight I did not expect to see today in my town.

Stefan Jackson stood clad in a leather jacket and dark jeans, glaring directly at Jack and me.

I was taken aback. When I was beginning to get him off my mind, he came back to stir things up.

My feelings were conflicted—part anger, part astonishment. My heart pounded in a way I didn't want to face.

Stefan looked dangerously hot.

I loathed myself for even contemplating him in that manner. He was the last person I should have been thinking about. Yet, there he stood, as real and impossible to disregard. He approached closer, his eyes and lips tightly pursed. He seemed cold and angry. His gaze was fixed on us with an intensity I could almost feel across the distance.

Jack observed the shift in my expression.

"I'm guessing that's the jerk," he muttered.

I nodded. "That's him."

Before I could say another word, he was on his feet.

"Relax, I've got this," I said, sounding braver than I felt. How did Stefan track me down?

Jack's eyes never left Stefan. "You sure?" he says.

"I don't like the way he's looking at you."

Jack's concern was obvious—he wasn't about to back down as Stefan strode toward us. This wasn't Jack's fight, but it was about to become his problem if I didn't intervene.

"I'm sure," I said, smiling reassuringly for Jack's sake.

He didn't seem entirely convinced, but he sat back down, his posture still tense, still watching Stefan like a hawk.

## Chapter Sixteen

# Abby

I took a deep breath and marched forward.

My heart pounded louder with every step toward Stefan. The closer I got, the thicker the tension became. Stefan's eyes weren't on me; his gaze was glued to Jack. It was apparent he was assessing the situation to determine his next move.

"What are you doing here?" I asked.

"I wanted to see you so we could talk," he says.

He threw another glance at Jack before turning back to me.

"Who is he? What are you doing with him?"

"Who I'm with is none of your business. Who made you the CEO of my personal life?"

He looked shocked, but I didn't care. I'll give him answers if he wants, although they may not be what he wants to hear.

His face was hard, and I could hear his breathing as he stood before me. I felt overwhelmed by his presence, which seemed to fill the space between us. One sniff of his scent, and I instantly tensed up.

"Come with me," he pleaded.

"No!" I retreated, snatching my arm away when he reached for it. "Go back, Stefan. I don't want to see you."

"Please, Abby, I'm begging you, give me five minutes and I'll leave."

His stare grew heavy just as Jack stood behind me.

"Is there a problem here?"

I turned to see Jack standing with his hands at his sides, his stance wide, his eyes scanning protectively, and his jaw set in a way that indicated he wouldn't back down.

"Back off, who the hell are you?" Stefan asks with irritation.

Jack didn't flinch. He didn't look away. Instead, he stepped toward Stefan, his eyes locked onto Stefan's with an intensity that nearly matched his own.

"What if I don't?" Jack challenged.

"Then I'll make you."

I felt the situation spiraling. I wasn't sure what Stefan was doing here, but I knew the last thing I needed was to be caught in some weird standoff between him and Jack. It was stupid, and I wouldn't let it get out of hand.

I moved between them, my hands raised to de-escalate the situation. "Guys, stop," I said, my tone stern as I looked from Jack to Stefan. "Jack, I'll talk to you in a minute. Just… please, let me handle this."

I grabbed Stefan's arm, tugging him away from Jack. He didn't pull away, but the look in his eyes told me he wasn't ready to let it go.

I turned to Jack and said, "Give me a moment, I'll be right back.

Jack looked between us, not saying anything else, and nodded as he sat back on the bench.

As I walked away with Stefan, I could feel my patience wearing thin.

"Why are you here, Stefan?" "And what do you want? I'm doing my best not to cause a scene in public."

"I'm not here to cause trouble," he muttered. "But I didn't expect to see you with some guy."

"Why do you care?" I shot back. "You don't get to control who I spend time with. We are nothing to each other, remember?"

"I don't want to argue with you," he said quietly. This was unlike his usual cockiness. "I just..." He trailed off, leaving the sentence unfinished.

I scoffed. Typical. Of course, he doesn't know what he wants.

I returned to Jack to inform him that I would call later.

As I headed home, I heard Stefan's footsteps behind me. I tried to keep my cool as my nerves went haywire. Once I arrived home, I made sure to shut the door. Then, there was a knock at the door.

"Can we talk, please?"

I swung the door open so fast that I spun around, nearly tripping. My hands clenched into fists at my sides.

"What the hell are you doing here?"

"Did you think everything would be fine again just because you showed up? That I'm just going to—what? Forget everything?"

Stefan stood a few feet away, his face unreadable and his jaw tight. The lack of response only fueled my anger. "Are you just going to stand there and look at me like that?" I shouted. "Or are you here to have more fun?"

He stepped forward, and my breath hitched. My chest rose and fell rapidly.

"I deserve that." He says.

"Why are you in my house right now?"

He remained silent. Naturally, he chooses to be quiet when I need him to speak.

"You know what? Just leave. I don't need this. I don't need you—"

Suddenly, my back was pressed against the house wall with a soft thud. My breath caught in my throat, my heart raced, but it wasn't fear. No, this wasn't fear. Something else twisted in my stomach, something I shouldn't be feeling.

His hands gripped my arms, pressing me firmly against the wall. I looked up at him, my breath shallow, my pulse hammering in my ears. His face was so close. I felt his head in the crook of my neck.

"I'm sorry, Angel."

For a moment, everything went still. The words I had been screaming, anger, and confusion, all just... stopped.

Come on, react, I fought with my inner thoughts. This wasn't supposed to happen, and I shouldn't be liking this. I'm supposed to push him away. Then it happened: Stefan's lips crushed against mine without another word. My entire body lit up with an electric rush. My heart skipped, and in that instant, nothing else mattered. There was only the heat of his kiss, taste, tongue—so familiar, so intoxicating.

# Chapter Seventeen

## Stefan

This wasn't the apology I'd rehearsed in my head, but damn it, the second I saw her with that guy, I knew letting her go wasn't an option. For the first time in my life, I wanted something more serious. Something not even my parents could script for me. When she asked why I was there, I wanted to say, "I'm here for you," but the words tangled somewhere between my heart and mouth.

When she told me she didn't need me, I knew I had to do something-anything-because the thought of her being with him was unbearable. So, I did the only thing that made sense in the moment: I pinned her against the wall, every last bit of restraint dissolving. One breath of her scent, and I was a goner. Possessed. Her body against mine was the only cure I craved, and her lips were the antidote to all my problems.

I swear, I lose all control when I'm with her. I pulled back just enough to meet her eyes, searching for a sign. My gaze dropped to her lips—God, how I missed them. I knew this wasn't the time or place, but I had to kiss her just once more, in case she decided she was done with me for good. When our lips finally met, it was electric. She hesitated at first, but didn't push me away. When she kissed back, I was drowned in relief. My lips grew insistent, desperate, hungry to make up for lost time.

She moaned softly, sending blood rushing straight to my pants. I craved another taste of her, a memory to hold onto if this were all I'd get. When we broke apart, breathless, something inside me detonated. I didn't want to stop. My hands found the hem of her sweater, desperate to feel her skin, to erase the pain I had caused and replace it with something worth remembering.

"Can I?" I asked.

She nodded, her lips parting just enough to release a soft sound that was like music to my ears. I paused, my hand hovering an inch above her skin, waiting for any sign of uncertainty. But her hungry gaze drew me in.

My fingers glided slowly up her sides, landing on her breasts, which are perky and just the right handful. She shivered beneath my touch. Abby pressed closer, her hips rolling against my thigh, her breath growing uneven. I let my hand wander, relishing the heat her body emitted. I could feel her muscles tensing and relaxing beneath my palm.

Her arched eyelids fluttered, and a curse slipped out as I slid my hand beneath the waistband of her jeans. The fabric felt damp, her need unmistakable. I gulped as her heartbeat grew louder in my ears, torn between wanting to push further and needing to draw this out just a little longer.

A tremor ran through her as I found her rhythm; she bit her lip to stifle a moan. Her head fell back. My own need pressed tightly against my jeans, but I held back, savoring the anticipation as the tension between us thickened.

She gasped my name, her voice ragged as I leaned in and brushed my lips against her ear. "You missed this dick?" I murmured, letting the question hang between us.

"I miss your tight pussy; can I fuck you?" I must have sounded needy.

Her only response was a desperate nod, wordless yet impossibly clear.

She reached for my jeans, her fingers fumbling with the clasp before easing the zipper down. Determined to get off, her hand slipped into the slit of my boxer briefs to free me. Her touch shocked me. I sucked in a breath, pulse pounding, impatient I helped her slide my jeans and boxers down.

She stilled, her eyes widening in surprise as I stood at attention.

"You can take it."

My resolve snapped, and without a thought, I turned her toward the wall, pressing her palm flat against it, while my other hand traced the curve of her back. Breathless, she gasped, and I felt every nerve ending in my body light up.

"You have no idea how irresistible you are." I was unable to tear my gaze away from her. Her body was art—every line and curve drew me in, making restraint feel impossible.

My hands shook as I fished a condom from my pants pocket on the floor. What a view her ass was, I kiss both cheeks before tearing open the condom with a practiced flick.

"You just knew you were going to have your way with me, huh?" she teased.

I grinned and pressed my lips to her shoulder. "Let's just say I like to be prepared."

She laughed, "Whatever, Boy Scout."

"I'm sorry—I can't help myself," I whispered. I slid into her slowly, and her body welcomed me. Both of us gasped as the tension finally broke.

She bit her bottom lip, stifling a moan, her hands pressed against the wall. The heat between us was stimulating; every movement drew us closer.

I released her hand, my grip tightening around her waist as I moved faster, our bodies found the beat that felt both urgent and inevitable. I pressed my lips to her neck, murmuring, "You feel incredible."

She arched against me, her breath coming in short, desperate bursts. "Right there, don't stop," she pleaded.

Her body tightened around me, her hips moving in time with mine until she cried out, her release sending me over the edge. I caught her as her legs gave out, holding her close as we both shuddered, breathless.

For a moment, we remained like that. Her head on my chest, my arms wrapped around her.

"You're so beautiful," I whispered, brushing her hair from her face. "I want you in my life."

She relaxed against me, her heartbeat slowing, and I held her as if letting go would mean losing everything I'd just discovered.

Afterward, we cleaned up together, our playful touches easing the intensity.

Clarity struck me in the silence that followed. But I meant every word. I would no longer run from what I felt.

But her reaction wasn't what I'd hoped for. She tensed in my arms. "I'm so stupid," she says, trying to slip from my embrace. My heart plummeted.

"Abby, please, don't pull away," I murmured, holding her tighter, desperate to keep her close. "I never meant to hurt you. I was an idiot, scared of how fast everything was moving, scared of how much I felt for you. I know I messed up, but I can't lose you. Please, give me a chance to prove I'm worth your trust again. If you can't forgive me, I'll understand. I just... I couldn't live with myself if I didn't tell you the truth. What we have is real. I swear, Abby. I like you more than I've ever wanted anyone.

She spun around in my arms; her face streaked with emotion and her eyes shining with unshed tears. I felt vulnerable as she stared into my eyes.

Neither of us spoke. The only sound was the thumping of our hearts as we sat waiting for whatever came next.

"Are you lying to me?" she whispers.

I shook my head, my gaze unwavering. "Never. If I ever made you feel that way, you have my full permission to slap me. Honestly, seeing you sad is the worst punishment I could get."

A single tear slipped down her cheek. I caught it with my thumb, wishing she could see how much I meant it. I pressed a gentle kiss to the cheek, and her tears fell, lingering there.

Her voice cracked. "Don't lie to me, please."

"I won't. I swear, I never want to hurt you again." My words were soft and honest as I meant every one of them. "I want us to start over. I hate that our relationship began with a silly dare. But I promise, every moment since then has been real.

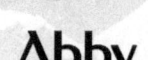

# Chapter Eighteen

## Abby

The house is quiet when I hear the door open and Mom's key turning in the lock. I sat up, startled, realizing I was tangled in Stefan's arms. Thank God I had the presence of mind to put on our clothes earlier.

"Stefan," I whisper-shout, shaking him lightly.

"Hm?" He stirs, yawning.

I heard her footsteps in the hallway as she made her way to the living room. I look up to find her standing there.

"Hi Mom," I say, hoping she couldn't sense what we did.

"Abby," "What are you doing so late in the living room?" She reaches for the light switch and notices Stefan then, and her eyebrows rise in question. "And... who is this?"

I feel my cheeks flush even harder, and I glance at Stefan, unsure how to introduce him. He quickly understands what's happening and sits up.

"Mom, this is Stefan, my friend."

"And Stefan, this is my mom, Melissa." Stefan stands up, extending a hand toward her. "Nice to meet you, Mrs.

McKenna." He says it smoothly, but I can hear the slight nervousness beneath his words.

Mom gave him a long look and then glanced at me, as if silently asking me for some explanation. The silence felt awkward and uncomfortable.

She finally shakes his hand. "Nice to meet you," she says, her eyes scrutinizing him.

"I'll be right back," I told Mom, encouraging Stefan to follow me.

His gaze flickered between my mom and me. "I'll be...." He gestured to me.

I was relieved to see him retreat upstairs. I turned back to Mom, who was watching us. After showing Stefan my room, I came back downstairs.

"Abby, what's this about?" "Why is that young man in my house?"

I swallow, unsure of what to say. She would have met Stefan eventually, but I didn't expect her to meet him now, especially not under these circumstances.

"I'm sorry, Mom. I didn't expect him to show up here," I say.

"Is everything okay?" She asks with concern.

"I'm not sure," I answered quietly. I didn't want her to have a bad impression of Stefan before getting to know him. "I like him mom. Like a lot, I do."

"Ah, that's what this is." Mom's expression relaxes, and she looks at me with a much softer gaze. "Now that's a relief. I thought you were being abused or was in some trouble." She gives me another look over before asking again, Are you sure?"

"Yes, Mom, I want to ensure you're not doing something you'll regret."

"Why would I regret it?" I ask, confused.

Her brow furrows. She steps closer, a hint of sadness in her eyes. "No. But sometimes, people seem different, only for things to turn out the same way."

Her words hang in the air, heavy and laced with concern. I know what she's referring to. I've tried not to think about it, wanted to bury it beneath the surface of my emotions—the way my father left us without any explanation, the abandonment that still lingers in the back of my mind, the shadow of it constantly creeping in.

"I don't know," I admit. "But I'll try to figure it out. That's why I came home. It's not just about him, it's... everything. I've had so much weighing on me, and I needed to clear my head."

She watches me closely, filled with concern. "I understand," she says finally, her tone softening. "But just remember, Abby, that your heart is yours to follow. Don't let what happened with your father guide your decisions. You're stronger than that."

I swallow hard, feeling a lump in my throat. "I don't want to make the same mistakes twice."

Her expression softens. She steps forward, pulling me into a tight hug. I let myself sink into it, the warmth of her embrace making me feel safe.

"You won't," she says firmly. "And whatever happens with Stefan, you will make the right choice. I'm proud of you, Abby. Just let your heart lead."

I nod against her shoulder, grateful for her support. "Thanks, Mom."

We pull apart, and I can see the tiredness in her eyes. "Get some rest, sweetheart. We'll talk more later. Good night."

"Good night," I say softly as she heads upstairs. Mom means well, and she's just looking out for me. But I also know she doesn't understand my pull toward Stefan. It's more than just attraction, more than just a fling. It feels real, even though it scares me.

With a deep breath, I turned and headed upstairs. When I reached my room, I found Stefan sitting on the edge of the bed, his back to me, looking at my photos and awards. His shoulders were tense, and his body language was rigid. He must have heard the conversation downstairs.

I close the door quietly behind me and walk over to the bed, standing in front of him for a moment, unsure of what to say.

Stefan looks up, his eyes meeting mine, and I see a trace of worry in his expression. "I messed up, didn't I?"

I smile a little, shaking my head. "No," I say, sitting beside him. "It wasn't like that. It's just... my mom's protective."

He exhales and rubs the back of his neck. "I wasn't trying to make things weird," he says, his voice sincere.

"I know," I reply, with a small smile. "I'm... I'm trying to figure things out. But it's hard."

He leans over and gently kisses my nose, the touch light and tender. He pulls me into his arms, and I relax against him, the steady beat of his heart beneath my ear throbbing. We don't say anything more; the quiet room and the constant rhythm of our breathing are enough.

# *Chapter Nineteen*

## Abby

Stefan's warmth enveloped me as he lay beside me, his arm draped over my waist. I tried not to dwell on how much I would love waking up like this daily. I released a happy sigh, grateful that Stefan had come after me. How I wish time would stop so we could bask in this moment. Far away from all the noise on campus.

I shifted slightly to face him, and our eyes locked. A slow smile gradually spread across his face.

"Morning," he murmurs. And damn, his husky morning voice stirred something inside me.

"Morning," I whisper back, unable to suppress the flutter of warmth in my chest.

He leaned in and pressed a chaste kiss on my forehead and lips. I felt the pulse of affection in his touch, reminding me of how much I didn't want to leave and dreaded facing school, finals, and everything waiting for me back there.

But I know I have to go. Graduation is approaching, so I couldn't prolong my stay. Plus, I have two people waiting for my return.

With a deep breath, I pull back slightly. "We should probably get ready to go back," I say.

Stefan looks at me, his expression warm. "Yeah," he presses another kiss, this time on my lips, before pulling away and reaching for the edge of the blanket to push it off us. The cool air makes me shiver slightly, and I sit up, rubbing my eyes.

"Do you want to take a shower together?" I suggested. He nodded eagerly, his eyes gleaming with enthusiasm.

Stefan stands up and stretches, his muscles rippling as he moves, and I can't help but watch him. Just seeing him fills me with desire. He catches me staring and winks, "Like what you see?" he asks smugly.

"I've seen better," I replied.

Looks like you need something in that mouth of yours. He grinned before grabbing me, putting me in the shower, and turning on the cold water.

"You mother fucker," I scream and pull him in with me before he can escape.

After a quick shower—no fooling around—especially with Mom at home—I remembered that he had left his car near the park. "Crap, I forgot to text Jack." I found my phone and saw his texts, as well as messages from Alexis and Jessica. I responded to his texts to let him know I was okay and that we would hang out later. I also sent a single text message to our group chat and continued getting dressed.

Stefan stepped outside to retrieve his car. I hoped that he and Mom would be okay. Even though I briefly discussed him yesterday, I still worry that she might feel cold toward him.

### Stefan

"Good morning, Mrs. McKenna," I began. "I want to apologize for getting off on the wrong foot. I am especially sorry for hurting Abby and for coming to your home unannounced. Please allow me to make it up," I say sincerely.

"Call me Melissa," she said, scanning my face. "Sit down," she ordered. I did as I was told and sat on one of the kitchen stools.

"Look, I don't know what happened between you two, nor do I want to know all the details. I'm going to trust my daughter to make her own decision. And hopefully it's the right one." "My concern is you. I don't know your relationship, but please make things clear with her. I don't want to see her hurt again."

"I'm sorry, I'm not good at expressing my feelings." I am working on that. The one thing I'm sure of is that I like her more than a friend. I caught a slight upturn of her lips before it faded away. I offered a polite smile in return.

"I will be watching," she stated.

"Thank you," I responded. "You have my word."

"You better, because if I find out you hurt her again, it won't be pretty," she said, handing me a cup of coffee.

### Abby

After getting ready, I headed downstairs to find Mom and Stefan engaged in deep conversation in the kitchen.

"Morning, Honey," she smiles when she sees me.

"Morning, Mom," I reply, sitting beside Stefan.

She gathers her things for work and informs me, "I'm running late. "I need to go, but I'll return later this evening. We'll talk then, okay?" "Stefan, I can tell you more stories later."

"I would love that," he said with a smirk.

My mouth dropped open. When had they become friends?

"About that, I'll be going back to school today," I tell her with a sheepish smile.

Her eyebrows raised. "Really? That soon," she asked.

Yeah, I have classes, and finals are approaching...

"It's alright, I don't have a problem with you leaving, I'm just saying that it's sudden," she pulls me into a hug. "We can still talk on the phone, right?"

I hug her back. "Of course,"

"Have a safe trip back, then. Both of you."

Stefan stands up and walks toward her.

"Thanks, Mrs. McKen... I mean Melissa," he says quickly. "I'll take care of her."

I feel the heat rush to my face as I watch my mom's reaction. She has a tender expression as she stared at Stefan before hugging him.

"You'd better," she says.

My mother has always fiercely protected me, which signifies her silent approval, even if she doesn't fully understand everything happening.

She gives me a quick hug. "Use protection, and don't make me a grandma just yet," she says before heading toward the door. "Take care of yourself, Abby."

We laughed and waved as she climbed into her car and backed out of the driveway. I felt the butterflies again as I turned back to Stefan. I was ecstatic that my mom was at least somewhat okay with him.

I walked over to him and wrapped my arms around his torso. I held him close, listening to the rapid beat of his heart, which sounded like a drummer performing a solo. He responded by kissing me gently on the head. Someone, please pinch me because this feels too good to be true.

We both head back upstairs, moving in sync as we gather and prepare to leave.

# Abby

The ride back feels much longer, even though Stefan is driving. Aside from our bathroom breaks, we've stopped several times to appreciate the scenery. We knew we needed to discuss our relationship, but for now, we enjoyed each other's company. The gentle sway of the vehicle was oddly comforting. Stefan held my hand as he drove, and I soon fell asleep.

When we finally returned to campus, I woke up to my heart sinking with silent dread.

"I'll text you," he says as if reading all my thoughts and insecurities.

I nod okay. A tight, nervous smile tugs at the corners of my lips. He shifts closer, his breath warm on my cheek as he leans in, brushing his lips against mine in a kiss that's so sweet it burns. I kiss him back, my heart thudding in my chest.

He reluctantly pulls away and gazes down at me, his longing mirroring my feelings.

"Don't forget to unblock me, please, so I can reach you," he says with his signature smirk.

I chuckled and gave him a small wave before quickly heading inside our dorm, noticing that we were being watched.

I walked into a relaxed room—Jessica was curled up on the couch, watching one of her romance dramas, while Alexis lounged on the opposite sofa, engrossed in her phone. Beside them lay their books.

Jessica glances up first. However, Alexis doesn't even look at me. She seems absorbed in her phone, but I notice her body tense up.

This is the moment I've been dreading all this time. They've been my rock through all of this, and I've just left them hanging while I've gone off to sulk and wallow in my mess.

"I, uh…" A massive lump in my throat made it hard to swallow, but I pushed forward. "I'm sorry. I was… at a bad place, and my emotions got the best of me."

Jessica paused her show and gave me her undivided attention. "I shouldn't have taken it out on both of you," I continued. Although you pushed me to try new things, I still had the choice to say no. I shouldn't have blamed you for everything." I know you meant well and have been supportive; I shouldn't have acted like that." The silence in the room held the words and the shame that crept up my spine as I admitted my mistakes.

Without another word, Alexis gets up and crosses the room toward me. She hugs me, her arms tight as if holding me together. Once again, I am shocked by her sudden affection, but then I melt into it. Choked up, I could feel the knots that had been twisted in my stomach since I'd left come undone.

"Never do that again, Abby," her words muffled against my hair. "We're here for you, no matter what. Don't push us away."

I'm sorry. I'm so, so sorry for everything. It won't happen again.

"I'm sorry too." "I shouldn't have pushed you too much," Alexis says.

Jessica gets up. "Me three." I should have stopped when you felt uncomfortable.

"It's okay," I replied.

"I want my hug, too," she says, pulling Alexis and me back for another hug. Her petite frame wraps around both of us as she snuggles into me.

"I'm glad you're back," Jessica chirped.

"Me too."

I allow myself to be held by my friends, and everything feels much better now.

We stand there for a moment, just holding each other, before Alexis pulls away first and quickly wipes away her tears. I feel bad that I made her cry.

"So… tell us what happened." She said.

I can't hide my blush as Jessica squeals, pulling me toward the couch. "Tell us everything."

As I settle back on the couch with them, the TV forgotten, I recount everything that happened.

"You know, he came to us apologizing and begging to talk to you," Jessica informed me with a hint of amusement. "He even brought flowers and a huge teddy bear."

"Really?"

"Oh, you should've seen his face," Alexis said, barely containing her laughter. "He looked so pitiful. I scolded and made him promise not to pull a stunt like that again, or else I'd kick him where it hurts."

I couldn't help but laugh, picturing the scene.

Alexis continued, her tone turning slightly sheepish. "I, uh... I shared your location with him. I'm sorry I didn't ask for your permission first."

That's how he knew where I was, I thought. I felt ecstatic. "It's okay. Thank you, both of you." I paused, feeling a surge of affection for my friends. "I love you guys."

"I love you, too," Jessica replied, a big smile on her face.

"Me too," Alexis added, her voice full of fondness.

It's finals week, and I'm barely hanging in there, buried by schoolwork—the pile of textbooks on my desk, the countless study sessions with Jessica and Alexis. So exhausted, I can barely keep my eyes open when midnight hits each night. It's so stressful. But somehow, despite it all, I'm still able to function.

Maybe it's because of Stefan. We've been calling and texting all through, with a bit of hanging out in between whenever we have free time. I never realized how much I needed this kind of companionship until now. Jack and I weren't even like this back when I dated him. Although we were much younger, our relationship was more of a friendship than a romantic or sexual one. It's all three at once with Stefan, and I can't get enough.

It's not just the late-night calls and texts that make me happy. It's everything. He makes me laugh with his ridiculous attempts to be "romantic," just because of flowers, the little head kisses, the way he sends me random memes when I'm stressed, and how he always asks about my well-being, even though we're both buried in books. And most importantly, the way he holds my hand in public despite Lisa and her insane friends' cruel behavior towards me. It's the little things. I'm starting to understand why I've been drawn to him and why my heart races whenever I see his new message. He's caring, which makes me like him a lot.

And then, there's the fact that he's making an effort. He's been studying too, but he makes time for me. Even on the nights when we're both too exhausted to do anything but stare at each other through the screen, it feels sufficient. Just knowing he's there is enough.

The more time passes, the more I realize I am not just having fun with him; I'm falling for him. In love with him. Okay, I'll stop rambling.

# *Chapter Twenty-One*

❀

# Abby

The sun shone brightly, and a gentle breeze blew as the colorful leaves waved at us. Alexis, Jessica, and I sat outside, enjoying our lunch break. The campus square buzzed with activity, with students lounging on the grass or hurrying to their next classes. I took a bite of my caprese sandwich; it was like an orgasm in my mouth. So good that I let out a low moan from the burst of flavors.

A cold shock coursed through my body, interrupting my intimate moment with my sandwich. Icy water streamed down my back, soaking my shirt and sending chills down my spine. I gasped and turned around to confront the culprit.

Lisa stood there, an empty water bottle in her manicured hand, her lips curled in a faux-apologetic smile. "Oops, I'm so sorry," she cooed, her voice dripping with insincerity. "I didn't see you there."

Before I could even respond, Alexis was on her feet, moving with speed and grace. She grabbed her bowl of cream chowder and poured it directly onto Lisa's perfectly coiffed head in one fluid motion.

Time seemed to slow as the thick, creamy soup splattered down Lisa's face, chunks of potato and celery clinging to her carefully applied makeup. Her shriek of outrage pierced the air, drawing the attention of everyone within earshot.

"You fucking bitch!" Lisa screeched, frantically wiping at her face, and only succeeding in smearing the mess further.

Alexis's face was a mask of innocence. "Oh my, I'm sorry," she said, mimicking Lisa's earlier tone. "My hands must have slipped. How clumsy of me."

"You'll regret this," she hissed. "I'm going straight to the Dean. You'll all be sorry!" Lisa continued promising retribution. With that, she spun on her heel and stormed off, her entourage of sycophants trailing in her wake, shooting us venomous glares.

As the drama unfolded, I became acutely aware of the gathered crowd. Whispers and pointed looks reminded me of the rumors circulating since Stefan and I started dating. Cruel words echoed in my mind: "What does he see in her?" "She's just a placeholder until he finds someone better." "She must be blackmailing him."

I pushed the thoughts away, trying not to let them affect me. Lisa and her friends were the worst offenders, constantly spreading gossip and attempting to undermine my relationship. But I refused to succumb to them. Over my dead body would I give them the satisfaction of seeing me rattled.

Jessica's concern broke through my thoughts. "Are you okay?" she asked, eyes scanning me for signs of distress. I managed a smile, "I'm fine," I assured her. "It's just water. No harm done."

A familiar voice cut through the crowd's murmur. "Well done!" it called out, accompanied by enthusiastic applause.

I turned to see Kevin, Mason, and Stef approaching, their grins plastered across their faces. They must have witnessed the entire spectacle.

Kevin's eyes were fixed on Alexis, admiration evident in his gaze. "Feisty," he remarked, clearly impressed by her quick thinking and bold action. I made a mental note to ask Alexis about that night at the club again; she had been evasive when I brought it up. I get the feeling that something happened between them after I left. There's always this tension between her and Kevin.

Stef's warm brown eyes locked onto mine; concern etched across his handsome features. "Angel, are you alright?" he called out, quickening his pace to reach me.

"I'm okay," I reassured him, but a shiver ran through me as the damp fabric clung to my skin.

Stef pulled his shirt over his head without hesitation, revealing his toned torso. He then slipped it over my head, gently guiding my arms through the sleeves. The fabric was warm from his body and carried his familiar scent of sandalwood, along with something uniquely his own.

Mason coughed subtly, eliciting laughter from our friends and curious glances from onlookers. "Whipped."

Stef shot him a glare. "Shut up," he retorted, but the smile tugging at his lips revealed his lack of real annoyance.

Turning to Alexis, Stef's expression became serious. "Thanks for having Abby's back," he said sincerely.

Alexis shrugged, a mischievous glint in her eye. "No worries. Lisa had that coming for a long time."

Stefan clapped his hands together, his smile returning. "Well, ladies, I think this calls for a celebration. Dinner is on me tonight."

Alexis and Jessica nodded enthusiastically, as they were never ones to turn down free food.

"I'm in," Kevin says quickly, his gaze darting to Alexis.

"Count me in, too," Mason added with a grin.

As we gathered our things and began the walk back to our dorms, I felt the tension from the confrontation dissipate. Surrounded by my friends and wrapped in Stef's shirt, I pushed thoughts of Lisa and her petty schemes to the back of my mind. With finals looming just a week away, I had far more critical things to focus on.

The incident, however, had revealed some underlying issues. As we walked, I couldn't help but reflect on the dynamics of the situation. Alexis and Kevin's budding attraction, the malicious rumors about Stef and me, and the pressure of upcoming exams contributed to the growing list.

I glanced at Stef, who caught my eye and gave me a reassuring smile. His unwavering support had been my anchor through gossip and academic stress. Yet, a small part of me couldn't help but wonder whether the constant negativity would eventually take its toll on our relationship.

Pushing those thoughts aside, I focused on the present moment—the beautiful fall weather, my friends, and the promise of a good meal. Whatever challenges lay before me, I knew I had a strong support system with which to face them.

As we approached the dorms, our conversation shifted.

"I swear, if I have to memorize one more organic chemistry reaction, my brain might combust," Jessica groaned dramatically.

"Tell me about it," Kevin chimed in. "I've been staring at calculus problems for so long, I'm starting to see derivatives in my sleep."

The repartee continued as we planned a group study session later in the week. Despite the stress of finals, there was a sense of camaraderie in knowing we were all together.

As we reached the entrance of my dorm building, Stefan pulled me aside for a moment. His eyes searched mine, revealing concern and affection in their depths.

He cupped my cheeks and asked, "Are you sure you're okay?" "I know Lisa and her minions have been giving you a hard time."

I leaned into his touch, drawing strength from his presence. "I'm fine, really," I assured him. "Their words can't hurt me as long as I know the truth about us."

"And what truth is that?"

"That what we have is real." "And it doesn't matter what anyone else thinks or says."

He leaned in and pressed a soft kiss to my forehead. It's one of my favorite kisses of his. Something about its gentleness gives me a sense of warmth and comfort.

"That's my girl." "Now, go get changed. We've got a celebratory dinner to attend, and I'd like my shirt back at some point," he says.

I laughed, and the last of the tension from earlier melted away.

"Or I can help you undress and get dressed."

"Or you can get a room," Kevin yells. Causing everyone to laugh.

My cheeks started to burn. I rushed to my room to change. I felt a renewed sense of determination. None of Lisa's petty schemes, whispers, and stares mattered. I had true friends, a supportive boyfriend, and my strength to rely on.

As I changed out of Stefan's shirt, I caught one last waft of his comforting scent before setting it aside. I was ready to face whatever came my way.

With a sigh and a smile, I picked out a fresh outfit and rejoined my friends.

# *Chapter Twenty-Two*

❀

# Abby

It's the last day of finals, and I can finally stop studying and rest my brain from overstimulation. I no longer need to cram for my undergraduate studies. My hands were shaky when I left the previous exam, and I could hardly remember what I had just written. It's like my brain has been on overdrive for the past weeks, and now that it's over, I feel so relieved and exhausted.

As I walk out of the building, squinting into the bright afternoon sun, I hear, "Hey, beautiful, can you spare me a minute?" "Sorry, I'm not interested," I say.

I turn around just in time to see Stefan jog up to me with a wide grin. He sweeps me off my feet and spins me around. My laughter bursts out, a mix of surprise and pure joy. I hang onto him, my feet dangling.

"Stefan!" I laugh, trying to catch my breath. "What are you doing? Put me down!"

But he doesn't, spinning me a little faster before gently setting me down on my feet again. I stood there momentarily disoriented but grinning like a fool.

"Sorry," he says with a playful glint in his eyes, wiping a stray lock of hair from my face. "I just couldn't help myself. We did it! Finals are over!"

"We sure did!" I say, still catching my breath. This is the lightest I have felt in weeks. I can finally breathe again, like the weight on my shoulders has dissipated.

"How did it go? How was your last exam?" Stefan asked.

"I think I did okay," I reply. "What about you?"

"It was alright," he says. "But I'm just glad it's over."

"Ditto," I can't believe we're about to graduate," I say.

"I don't know where the four years went." He says.

"Mostly in bed, I joked.

"Very funny," he replied, shaking his head.

I stopped talking when I noticed that people were watching us.

I've never been one for attention, and the idea of being the center of it always made me uncomfortable. But as I look around, noticing the whispers and sideways glances from students passing by, I'm not too bothered by it. I'm standing here with Stefan, someone who makes me happy, someone I can finally admit I've fallen for. And if people are staring, so what?

I turn to Stefan and smile, feeling a warmth that has nothing to do with the sun.

"I think I'm ready to get out of here," I say, grabbing his hand.

He clasped our hands, his thumb brushing over my knuckles. "Yeah. Me too. Let's get out of here. You hungry?"

I nod. "Starving."

We walk side by side toward the exit, and I walk with a bit of pep in my step, feeling like I can touch the sun.

I can't help but beam as Stefan leads me toward a booth. His hand is warm on my lower back, guiding me, and I smile. I remember our first date at the diner when I thought he was ashamed to be seen with me. But this is a public place, and he's openly touching and leading me. It's a small thing, but it matters to me. He's been a good boyfriend since our discussion and making things official. He told me he's never been affectionate, but somehow, I find that hard to believe. He doesn't shy away from showering me with attention and affection.

"Are you going to just stare at me all night?" Stefan teases, pulling me out of my thoughts.

"You have a problem with that?"

"Of course not. My body is yours to look at and touch."

I blushed as my grin widened. See, I'm beginning to get accustomed to his sweet tongue. I need to tone down my smile before my face becomes the Joker.

"I'm just admiring the view," I retorted.

"I mean, I can't blame you," he says, laughing. I roll my eyes.

A familiar, deep, and loud call cut through the noise of the diner.

"Well, well, well," Mason's voice rings out, followed by Kevin's chuckling. They both swagger up to our booth. Stefan sighs, shaking his head. "You guys have to stop following me around," Stefan mutters, with a deadpan stare, but I can see amusement flickering through his eyes.

Mason doesn't miss a beat. "We're here for the entertainment," he says, sliding beside me. "Haven't seen Stefan this way before."

"Yeah," Kevin says. He looked at Stefan with a devious smile. "Do you know you had our friend brooding over you. Wondering where you went? He was a mess, Abby."

Stefan's face immediately turns bright red. "Shut up," he says, nudging Kevin in the ribs. He stares down at his plate, refusing to look at anyone.

Mason glanced at me, eyes wide with mock innocence. "Oh, he won't tell you, but we will. Poor guy was walking around like a zombie, trying to win his girl back." He got closer and wrapped an arm around me. "It was hilarious, Abby. You should've seen him."

"Get your dirty hands off my girlfriend or else," Stefan threatened.

I can't help but grin. Stefan's embarrassment is amusing, but it's also endearing in a way that warms my heart.

"Well, I'm glad to hear he's been distressed," I snort. "It sounds like I've been on his mind."

Mason winks at me. "Oh, you have, believe me. He wouldn't shut up about you for days. 'What did I do?' 'Why did I mess things up?' And don't even start on how much he missed you."

Stefan groaned, his face a deep shade of crimson, pressing it into his palms.

Kevin adds, "Yeah, he was a total loser. I thought I'd have to take him to therapy or something. Maybe you should think about that, Abby."

I'm practically grinning from ear to ear by now, and Stefan glares at his friends, hands clenching around his cup.

I turn to him, my eyes dancing with mischief. "Wow, Stefan. Sounds like you were pretty worked up. Do you mind elaborating?"

Stefan doesn't respond, but I feel his foot crawl up my legs and stop. He looks up at me, his signature smirk in place. My breath catches. His eyes are dark and filled with unspoken promises. I swallowed, bit my lip, and tore my gaze away from him and back to his friends.

"Thanks for letting me know about that, guys," I say to Mason and Kevin, who are still smiling like two fools. "It's nice to hear he cares."

The two of them laugh, "We're happy to share, Abby," Mason says with a wink. "But you should know, we've got many more stories. We could sit here all day and discuss Stefan's most embarrassing moments. Trust me, there's a lot."

"For a fee, though," Kevin inputs. "Alexis's number, maybe?" he asks, clasping his fingers together.

I laugh. "I'll think about it."

Stefan cursed under his breath, still red in the face, rolling his eyes at them. "Alright, enough. You've had your fun."

Kevin and Mason chuckle and stand, not ready to let up yet. "Good luck, Steffie," Mason coos, puckering his lips at him as they walk away.

"I hate you both," Stefan groans. Once they leave, I look at Stefan, my grin still wide. "Well, that was fun."

He shifts in his seat, rubbing the back of his neck. "I hate those guys," he mutters.

"I guess I was a bit... out of sorts."

"I can tell Steffie," I tease, leaning in just a little closer, trying to make him squirm. "You've got it bad, huh?"

He raises an eyebrow, a flirtatious smile forming as he catches my gaze. "I do," he says but if you keep teasing me, I'm going to fuck it out of your memory," I felt his foot higher.

My core tightened at his words, and I fought against the shiver tracing down my spine. Before I could utter anything back, he leaned in, his tone low and serious. "You know, my parents would like to meet you."

My eyes widened. "Your... parents?" I repeat.

"Yeah. I know it's sudden, but they've been asking about you. And I want you to meet them."

I blink, trying to keep my composure. This feels like a big step. "Are you sure about that?" I stuttered.

"I'm sure. You're important to me, Abby. I want them to meet the person who's got me all...out of whack."

I swallow hard, and my emotions suddenly go into overdrive. I'm flattered, of course, but also... scared. Meeting your boyfriend or girlfriend's parents is already a lot. But my circumstances are worse.

I force myself to smile. "I guess I'm not really in a position to say no now, am I?" I chuckle nervously.

He laughs, "You can, but I would love for you to meet them."

"I'll think about it," I say, though deep down, I know I'll say yes.

Relieved, he grabs my hand over the table, releasing some tension.

# Chapter Twenty-Three

# Abby

My heart pounded as Stefan drove along the winding roads to his parents' house. The closer we got, the more my nerves spiraled out of control. I clutched the seatbelt in my lap, twisting my fingers and tying them into knots, just like my stomach feels. I don't know why I'm so freaked out. It's just his parents. And I've already met them, although I'm sure sneaking out of their son's bedroom wasn't the ideal first impression.

I sneaked a glance at Stefan, who looked as relaxed as if he wasn't driving me to a potential in-law tribunal. His hands rest comfortably on the wheel, tapping it gently. He looks handsome and unbothered in his green collared shirt. He caught my eye and flashed me a reassuring smile. I can see the faintest hint of amusement in his expression.

"Hey," he says, "You're gonna be fine. My parents are excited to meet you."

Excited? I doubted that was the word they'd use. "Are you sure?"

"Positive," he replied. "There's nothing not to like about you." He turned onto a street lined with houses so fancy, even the mailboxes looked like they cost several grand. "I know you are stressed because of who they are. "But despite my parents being straightforward and sometimes intense. They'll love you. Trust me."

"Yeah, well… I'm not so sure about that. I'm pretty sure sneaking out of their son's bedroom isn't a good look, you know?"

His smile faltered for a nanosecond, just long enough for me to know he remembered. "You're overthinking it. They're not going to judge you for that. If anything, they'll want to know more about the girl who has me all worked up."

I tried to believe him, but the knots in my stomach weren't entirely convinced. Who knows, I might get lucky, and I'll leave with their approval. Who was I fooling? At least this time, I can go without the walk of shame.

The car glides to a stop in front of a mansion like the one you see in movies. I was distracted by the sheer number of windows- seriously, is there a room for every day of the week? Stefan kills the engine and turns to me, "Ready?" he asks.

I nod, but let's be honest, I'm about as ready as it gets. "Yeah. Let's get this over with I said under my breath."

Stefan, ever the gentleman, hops out, circles the car, and opens my door. I take his hand, partly for support, partly because my legs have turned to linguine. We march up the palatial walkway, and I try not to trip over my own feet from nerves.

The door swings open, and there stands Olivia, Stefan's mom, looking stunning, her dirty blonde hair perfectly styled.

"Hello!" she smiles, her eyes immediately zeroed in on me.

"Hi Mom," Stefan says, but she's already giving me the once-over.

"And you must be Abby," she says warmly. "We've met, but you were in a hurry last time."

Of course, she remembers. Lord, grant me invisibility. "I apologize for last time. I mustered a smile that probably looked more like a grimace and stuck out my hand. "It's nice to meet you officially. I've heard so much about you. I see you everywhere."

She laughs, waves off my handshake, and pulls me into a surprisingly comforting hug. "Don't be silly. You're the star tonight! We can't wait to hear all about you and how you managed to turn my son into a lovesick puppy," she teases, steering us inside.

I blush so hard I'm surprised the chandelier doesn't start melting. "I'm flattered," I say, which is true, if by flattered you mean "mildly terrified but trying to play it cool."

"Dinner is almost ready," Olivia announces, gesturing to a dining table big enough to host a family reunion. Stefan pulls out my chair like a pro, and I sit, silently vowing not to spill anything or say anything weird.

So far, so good.

"Everything looks and smells amazing," I complimented as I channel my inner food critic.

Olivia looks pleased. "Thank you, dear. It's a family recipe. One of Stefan's favorites." I catch Stefan's eye, and he looks happy.

As I'm about to sit, in strides Robert, tall and broad. His salt-and-pepper hair is on point, and his presence is so commanding.

"Abby, I take it?" His silvery, pleasant voice made me feel at ease. Not knowing what to do, I extended my hand once again, "Yes, sir. It's nice to meet you."

He shakes my hand, and I make sure to shake firmly. "Nice to meet you, too. Please, have a seat. Dinner's about to be served."

We all sat, Olivia got ready to spearhead the night, asking questions that put everyone at ease. Meanwhile, Robert observes silently, taking mental notes.

Then comes the classic dinner table ambush, "How did you two meet?" Robert asks. My cheeks go redder than the wine. If only I could say, "Well, it all started with a dare and a questionable amount of peer pressure…" But Stefan, ever the hero, swoops in. "It's a long story. We first met during Freshman year in sociology, worked as partners, but didn't connect until Mason's party. The rest is history." I could kiss him, him-preferably under the table, where his parents can't see.

But Robert isn't done. He fixes me with a gaze that could melt steel. "So, Abby, what are your plans after college? What do you want to do with your life?"

I take a breath and imagine I am a TED Talk speaker. "Well, I'm studying literature. I'd love to become a teacher, preferably a professor, one day, and teach at the college level. I've always loved reading and analyzing books, and I think I'd enjoy passing that on to others."

Robert nods. "A professor, huh? That's good work. You seem like someone serious about her future." He shoots Stefan a look that says, "Take notes, son."

My nerves start to thaw. Stefan's hand finds my knee under the table, and I look at him. He gives me a small, reassuring smile that makes my heart do a happy little tap dance.

Olivia jumps in, "Tell us about your family, Abby. What are your parents like?"

I decided to be honest. "My mom is amazing. She's worked hard to give me the best opportunities as a sales rep in the medical field. She and I are close, and I look up to her. My dad... well, he's not really in the picture. He left when I was young."

Olivia and Robert looked at me sympathetically. "That must've been tough," she says.

I shrug, not wanting to spoil the mood. "It was, but I've got my mom. She's enough for me."

From there, the conversation flows more easily. No one brings up my dad again, which I appreciate. Robert even cracked a smile once or twice.

By the end of the night, I'm laughing and chatting with Stefan's parents, who turn out to be way cooler than I'd expected. They're kind, funny, and they seem interested in getting to know me. Stefan was right- miracles do happen.

As the evening comes to an end, I stand and say, "This has been lovely. Thank you for having me over." Olivia pulls me into another hug, and Robert smiles. "You're welcome anytime. Don't be a stranger," Olivia says.

Robert nods, and for the first time, his smile is aimed right at me. "It was nice to meet you, Abby. Have a good night."

I practically float out the door on a cloud of relief. Stefan holds the car door open, grinning like he knew it would all work out. "See?" he says, smug and proud. "I told you they would love you."

I roll my eyes but can't help smiling. "You were right this time."

# Chapter Twenty-Four

## Stefan

Dinner was great. Abby got along so well with my parents; it's honestly scary. She's smart, witty, and genuine. I saw how mom warmed up to her instantly. She laughed at Abby's dry sense of humor and took the time to get to know her. Though typically reserved, Dad seemed impressed by how well Abby held her own in conversations. Usually, they're guarded about the people I bring home, worried that they are just using me for my money, which is a valid concern, but I'm glad they opened up to Abby. It's comforting how she fits into my world like she belongs there.

I'm not used to caring what anyone thinks about my love life, especially my parents, because they are never happy with anything I do. But suddenly, here I am, wishing for a five-star Yelp review from Mom and Dad. Ever since Abby and I got together, their opinion has started to matter more to me.

We slip into my car, and the engine hums as I drive. Abby's beside me, wearing that serene smile that makes me wonder if she's actually meditating or just plotting her next comeback. I couldn't help but sneak a glance at her, the streetlights highlighting the faint outline of her profile.

"Did you have a good time?" I ask, breaking the comfortable silence. I wanted to know what her impression of Mom and Dad was.

She blinks at me, those big doe eyes wide with surprise. "Of course. Your parents are great."

I let out a sigh, "I'm glad. My mom took a liking to you fast." Which is saying something because she loves to interrogate new faces.

"Aren't all mothers?" Abby chuckles. What a beautiful laugh she has.

"I think I made a good impression," she says. Then, with a sly look, "Also, keep your eyes on the road. I prefer to get home in one piece, not a jigsaw puzzle."

"You don't? I thought you wanted more of you to go around," I tease, waggling my eyebrows. She laughs and smacks my arm—a small price to pay for her laughter.

"Stop messing around and keep your eyes on the road."

"Yes, ma'am." I squeeze her hand, and it fits perfectly in mine, as if it were custom-made. Like an epiphany, it hits me. I want to hold this hand forever.

We reached her building, and I got out and opened her door. "Thank you," she says with a curtsy. And gives me an amused, suspicious look.

"Are you always this much of a gentleman? Or are you just trying to get some?"

I grin, "Only when I'm really into someone. Besides, I didn't know you were on the menu tonight. I could go for dessert," I say, winking.

She smiled. I could see the crinkle in her eyes, the one that makes my heartbeat faster. "Goodnight, Stefan," she whispers, eyes flicking to my lips.

I lean in, heart pounding. "I love you," I say, and kiss her soft, juicy lips. When we break apart, she meets my gaze, cheeks flushed.

"I love you, too, Stefan."

My heart nearly exploded. "Goodnight," I whisper, not wanting to let go.

She waves and disappears inside, leaving me grinning like an idiot in the parking lot.

I finally said it! I let the cat out of the bag, and guess what? She feels the same way. As I drive, I realize Abby has officially taken over my brain. She's all I think about. I have no idea what's wrong with me. I wish I were driving us to our home instead of dropping her off at her dorm and leaving.

I walked through the door and found Mom and Dad on the couch in the living room. They both looked up as I entered. I'm sure they were waiting for me. I wasted no time before asking,

"So, what do you think of Abby?"

Mom smiles, all warmth and approval. "Abby's lovely, Stefan. I'm glad you're spending time with someone like her."

"She is," Dad adds, "She seems like a good fit for you. She's got a good head on her shoulders. Try not to screw things up."

I'm not sure how to do that, except to thank Dad. There's nothing like a little paternal pep talk to keep the ego in check. I shook my head.

Mom turns the spotlight on me. "How do you feel about her?"

"I like her." "She's... unapologetically her." She doesn't want to change me-and, honestly, she makes me want to be better."

Dad observed me intently. "That's something."

I'm comfortable with her—the way she makes me feel like I'm more than just the playboy everyone thinks I am. Not to mention, she encourages me to approach things in a different way. Abby makes things complicated and straightforward at the same time.

I decided to go all in. "I told her I loved her today, and she said it back. I think I'm ready to take the next step." I rub the back of my neck, bracing for impact. "I think she's the one."

There's a long silence. Mom and Dad exchange looks, and I see their puzzled expressions.

Dad raises a brow. "Are you sure, Stefan? Marriage is a big commitment. And so soon..."

I get it. It sounds impulsive, but for once, I'm certain. "I know it seems fast, but Abby's different. I want this. I can't imagine her with anyone else-or me, for that matter. She's already worked her way into my heart."

My mom exhales sharply, "Stefan, is she pregnant?"

"Mom, no, this isn't a shotgun proposal."

"Then what's the rush?" she presses. "You barely know each other. How do you know she's not after your assets?"

"Mom!" I groan. "You just met Abby- does she strike you as a gold digger?"

She shakes her head, but she's not done. "Some people are good at pretending. You've never talked like this before. Now you're talking marriage after a few months?"

I can't help but laugh bitterly. "You two have been on my case for years about taking things seriously, about finding someone real. Now that I do, she's suddenly suspect?"

"Son, your mom means well. We want the best for you."

I sigh as disappointment settles in. For once, I thought I'd finally cracked the code and brought home someone I love, thinking they'd approve of. It turns out nothing I do will ever be right.

# Chapter Twenty-Five

## Abby

The door had barely clicked behind me before Alexis and Jessica pounced on me—two PJs-clad detectives, armed with a burning need for details.

"How did it go?" Jess demanded, her eyes wide as full moons.

I could use a moment to process, but that wasn't an option. "Someone, please pinch me. I must be dreaming," I muttered.

"Ouch!" I yelped, as Alexis obliged a second later, as someone who's been waiting all night for this.

"Good, now you know you're awake," Jess says smugly. "Now spill."

"Yeah, you're killing us!" Alexis added.

"Stefan told me he loves me. And... I said it back."

Cue the synchronized shrieks. I was still half convinced I'd wake up and find this was all a hallucination, but with that scream, I was sure I was awake.

"I'm so happy your feelings are reciprocated," Jess said.

"I know, right?" Alexis chimed in, clutching a pillow on her lap.

"OMG, I'm about to cry!" Alexis sniffled, eyes glistening.

I snapped out of my surreal moment for a second and turned my attention to Alexis. "Are you okay?"

"What do you mean?" Alexis replied, dabbing at her eyes.

"You've been… extra emotional lately. Not that it's bad! I want to make sure you're okay."

She glanced at Jess, who gave her a nod that seemed to say, 'Go on,' as if secretly communicating.

"It's okay if you don't want to tell me."

Alexis took a shaky breath, then blurted, "I'm pregnant," before promptly hiding behind her hands.

I froze. Did she say—? I looked at Jess, who nodded, confirming that this was not a prank.

I did the only thing I could, scoot closer and pulled Alexis into a hug.

### Three Months Later – Graduation Day

#### *Abby*

The spring air is fresh and flowery. As I sit squished between Alexis and Jessica on the bleachers, three matching graduation gowns, three sets of nerves, and at least one secret stash of tissues (thanks, Alexis). In less than two hours, we'll be college graduates, allegedly ready to face the world even though I still don't know how to fold a fitted sheet.

It's surreal—one minute, graduation was a distant neon sign, and now it's here, blaring in high-def. I want to freeze-frame these little moments: the late-night study sessions, the roommate coffee banter, the gossip that could power a small city. It's all playing in my head like a greatest hits reel, and I can't help but get emotional.

Jessica's already getting misty-eyed. "Can you believe it's finally here? We've talked about this day for years, and now it's happening. The reality is sinking in." Alexis grabs my hand, and I whip out my emergency napkin, ready for the waterworks. She laughs, sniffling, "I still can't believe I got knocked up in college. This was not on my vision board, at least not for another four to five years, when I'm a Jr. Associate."

"Life doesn't always go as planned. Please take all of our stories as an example. But look where we are now." I dab her tears, careful not to smudge her mascara. You're right," she says. I still think you should tell him."

"Agreed, it's his child too, please think about it," Jessica interjected.

"I will Alexis said quickly, changing the topic. "Are you sure you can't tell?"

"You can't tell." Jess and I reply in unison. I've lost count of how many times she has asked us this. She wanted to make sure her baby bump wasn't noticeable.

"Ready to strut across the stage and collect your costly piece of paper?" I joked.

"Hell yeah, I'm ready," Alexis says, sounding more confident than ever.

Of course, graduation has to separate us alphabetically, because nothing says "real world" like bureaucracy. We say our teary goodbyes and shuffle off to our departments.

As I walk, I wonder: Am I ready? I've spent the majority of my four years hiding behind textbooks, dodging drama, and following rules like they were gospel. But this last year of college changed me. I found confidence, took risks, and the major plot twist—fell in love.

Thinking of him, I get that warm, fizzy feeling, like my insides are a shaken soda. We've had our share of messes and misunderstandings, but we've learned to work through them.

My group is called to line up, and suddenly, my stomach hurts from nervousness and excitement. What if I trip and faceplant in front of the entire graduating class? What if I become a meme before I even get my diploma? I shake off the mental image. I took a deep breath and reminded myself: walk, don't wobble.

Then my name booms through the speakers—People clapped. Followed by a few shrieks. My heart was in my ass, and tears prickled at the corners of my eyes. I glue on my bravest smile and strut toward the stage.

At the podium, I scan the sea of faces for my mom. There she is, eyes sparkling, Jack beside her, grinning. And he who should not be named is nowhere to be found. But Mom-my rock, my hype woman, my everything. Seeing her so proud makes all the hard work worthwhile. I'm handed my diploma, which is a temporary placeholder. I strike a pose for the camera and prepare to make my exit.

Suddenly, there's a commotion downstage, and my brain immediately imagines disaster—fire? Streaker? Or perhaps even worse, a shooter?

But then I hear it: "Abby!" I whip around and spot Stefan marching toward the stage in his cap and gown. Did I forget something? I wondered.

Just as I'm about to say, "What are you doing?" he appears, stealing the spotlight and my breath.

"Abby," he says, voice ringing out over the crowd, "I know I've made mistakes, but what I feel for you—I've never felt for anyone else. I love you. And I want to spend every moment proving it."

The audience gasps. My heart is beating so rapidly that I thought I would have a heart attack. And then, in true rom-com fashion, Stefan dropped to one knee, his eyes locked with mine as he popped open the gray velvet box, which revealed a stunning teardrop diamond ring.

"Abby McKenna," he said lovingly, "will you marry me and start this beautiful new chapter of our lives together?"

I'm seconds away from sobbing in front of everyone, but I manage to say, "Yes! I'll marry you."

He slides the ring onto my finger, sweeps me up, and kisses me as if we're the only two people in the universe. The crowd goes wild. I think I hear someone yell, "Best graduation ever!"

As Stefan carries me off the stage, he whispers, "I love you, Mrs. Jackson." I grin, tears finally spilling over. "I love you, Mr. Jackson."

Let the world gossip. Let them judge. I'm not looking back; I'm walking into the future, diploma in one hand, Stefan in the other, my mom and best friends by my side, and not a single regret in sight.

## Epilogue

*Three Years Later*

### Third Person POV

Stefan Jackson stood in a side room, adjusting his tie in front of a large mirror. His reflection stared back at him, and though his usual confidence was present, he felt nervous, as if they were playing a final game at home and he had to win.

"How are you holding up, Coach?" Mason asked.

"I'm not nervous. Just… anxious."

Mason raised an eyebrow. "Yeah, sure. You've only checked that tie ten times since I got here."

Stefan rolled his eyes but laughed anyway. "It's not every day you marry the love of your life."

"True," Mason agreed, walking over to pat him on the back. "You've got this, man. If anyone can pull this off, it's you and Abby. Your whole story proves that crazy starts can lead to amazing endings."

"Amen to that!" Kevin says, joining the conversation.

Stefan smiled; it was true. Their story had been anything but conventional—a dare that should have resulted in a one-night encounter turned into a love neither of them could have predicted. Now, three years after graduation, he stood on the brink of marrying the woman who had turned his life upside down in the best possible way.

"Can I have a moment with Stefan?" Robert asked.

"Yes."

"Of course."

Kevin and Mason excused themselves. Robert stood in front of him. "Let me, he said, reaching to fix Stefan's tie. Son, I remember when your biggest worry was scraped knees and broken toys. Today, you step into a new kind of bravery, one that allows you to love, lead, and build a life with someone by your side. I know I may not say this often, but I am proud of you."

Stefan couldn't remember the last time he heard those words from his father. He almost forgot how much he needed them.

Across the hall, Abby McKenna stood in front of a mirror in her Bridal Suite, clutching her bouquet while her mom adjusted the hem of her dress.

"You look beautiful, sweetheart," Melissa complimented, stepping back to admire her daughter.

Abby turned to look at her mother, her eyes glistening with unshed tears. "Thanks, Mom. I still can't believe this is happening."

"You deserve happiness, Abby. You've worked so hard and found someone who loves you for exactly who you are. I couldn't be prouder." She said dotingly.

Abby bit her lip to keep from crying and hugged her mom tightly. As they pulled apart, Alexis and Jessica burst into the room, their blue bridesmaid dresses swishing as they entered. The man of honor, Jack, sauntered in, smiling ear to ear. "You look stunning," he praises.

"Thanks," Abby replied, smiling as she caught him staring at Jessica.

"Are you ready?" Alexis asked excitedly.

"She's more than ready," Jessica said, her smile warm and encouraging. "Stefan's the one who should be nervous."

Abby laughed, her nerves settling a bit. Her friends always knew exactly what to say.

"Just one more thing," Olivia, Stefan's mother, announced calmly as she entered the room. In her hand was a sleek black box that she held with care. Abby turned to her, curiosity piqued, as Olivia approached.

"This," Olivia began, opening the box to reveal a pair of beautiful pearl earrings, their luster timeless and elegant. They are your 'something old.' These earrings have been in our family for generations. My great-grandmother first wore them, followed by my nana, mother, and me on my wedding day. And now," her voice cracked, "I'm passing them down to you."

Abby's breath caught as she stared at the earrings, and her heart swelled at the significance of the gesture. "Olivia... I don't even know what to say," she whispered.

"You don't have to say anything," Olivia replied warmly, her eyes glistening as she placed the earrings in Abby's hands. "You are family now, and I couldn't be happier to see these worn by someone who means so much to Stefan and us."

Abby blinked back tears. "Thank you," she managed, gratitude shining through as she clutched the earrings. "This means so much to me. Truly."

Olivia leaned in and gave Abby a gentle hug. "You are such a beautiful bride," she congratulated, admiring her soon-to-be daughter-in-law.

Abby tilts her head back to prevent her tears from falling, filled with joy from the love and acceptance of her new family.

She replaced her earrings and took one last look in the mirror. Her dress was perfect—she was sure that's what every other bride said about their wedding dress. But hers was indeed perfect. I mean, how many people get to wear a custom-made wedding gown designed specifically for them, and the cherry on top, by their soon-to-be mother? Her dress is elegant, simple, and entirely her own. She looked like herself, just elevated, and that was exactly how she wanted.

"Let's do this."

The ceremony space was breathtaking. Rows of white chairs lined the aisle, adorned with flowers in soft pastels and bold blue hues. Friends and family filled the room, their faces glowed with happiness as they awaited the start of the wedding.

Stefan stood at the altar, flanked by Mason and Kevin, who grinned like fools. As the music began to play, the doors at the back of the hall opened, revealing Abby, with Melissa holding her hand.

Time seemed to stand still. Stefan's breath caught in his chest as he watched her walk toward him. She was radiant; her smile lit up the room, and for a moment, he forgot that anyone else was there.

Abby's eyes met his, and his nerves melted away. Nothing else mattered as she focused on the man waiting for her at the end of the aisle—a man who had supported and loved her in ways she never thought possible.

When she reached the altar, Melissa stepped forward, gently taking Abby's hand and placing it in Stefan's. Her gaze locked on his, warm yet serious. "Take care of her," she urged.

Stefan met her eyes, his own filled with quiet determination. "I will," he replied reassuringly. The moment hung between them, a silent promise exchanged. Without realizing it, Stefan lifted Abby's hand to his lips and gently kissed it. The gesture was instinctive and tender, drawing awe from the crowd. The officiant cleared his throat pointedly, breaking the spell. Abby and Stefan glanced up, their faces flushed.

The officiant began the ceremony, but all Abby and Stefan could focus on was one another. When it was time for their vows, Abby went first.

### Abby Vows

"Stefan," she began, her voice honeyed as she spoke. "When I think about how we started, I can't help but laugh. A dare. That brought us together—a silly, reckless game that was supposed to be meaningless. Somehow, it became something fruitful. You taught me to take risks, step outside my comfort zone, and truly live. You perceived me in ways I didn't even recognize myself, and showed me what it means to love and be loved without hesitation or fear. "I never imagined a single night could lead to a lifetime, but here we are. I promise to spend the rest of my days learning and experiencing life with you. I love you, Stefan. Always.

Stefan's jaw tightened as he fought back tears. Despite his efforts, tears streamed down his face. When it was his turn, he took a deep breath, and emotion was evident in every word he spoke.

### Stefan Vows

"Abby," he squeezed her hands gently. "I've always been confident, sure of myself, and ready for anything. But you shook my world in ways I never saw coming.

You challenged me, Abby, in the best ways. You made me work for your trust and heart, and I wouldn't change a second of it.

"I love you for your strength, kindness, intelligence, and the way you make me feel like the luckiest man alive just by being near you. I promise to love you, provide for you, and, most importantly, never to stop making you laugh. Although it all started with a dare, it was the best decision of my life."

Then, the officiant delivered the words everyone was waiting for.

"By the power vested in me, I pronounce you husband and wife. Stefan, you may kiss your bride."

Stefan pulled Abby close, their lips meeting as the crowd cheered. The kiss was deep, filled with love, joy, and a promise of forever.

As they walked back down the aisle together, hand in hand, the world appeared brighter, and the future felt limitless.

A reminder that what begins as a dare might be fate's way of nudging you toward someone you never realized you needed.

# THE END.

# Acknowledgment

The idea for Abby and Stefan's story came to me while I was deeply engaged with two other projects, both set for release in early 2025. Determined to stay on track, I quickly jotted down my thoughts and returned to those projects. However, their story remained persistent in my mind, refusing to be set aside. Eventually, I gave in and decided to bring *It All Started With A Dare* to life, shaping it into a novella whenever I could find some spare time.

A huge thanks to Nat Violet for taking the time to read and offer valuable feedback, and to my editor Emily for your incredible work as always.

To everyone else who contributed to making this book possible, thank you from the bottom of my heart. I couldn't have done it without you.

# About the Author

It All Started With A Dare is A.B. Holton's third novel. She has always been a hopeless romantic, finding joy in reading both fiction and non-fiction, and is amazed by the ability to explore different worlds from anywhere. After countless stories left her wishing for alternate endings, she took matters into her own hands and began writing her own.

Beyond writing, A.B. enjoys traveling the world with her husband and baking delicious treats. Writing a book has always been on her bucket list, and now she's turned that dream into a reality.

# Sign Up for A.B.'s Holton News Letter!

Keep up to date with A.B.'s Holton latest news on book releases and events by signing up for her email list at abholton.com.

## You May Also Like ...

HARPER THOMAS IS a devoted wife. Happily married to Ethan, her college sweetheart for almost five years, their life together appears perfect. However, a single text message threatens to unravel the life they have built together. The revelation forces Harper to confront the harsh reality behind their "Shattered Vows." Can the damage be mended, or are some betrayals beyond redemption?

## Learn More At:

 abholton.com

 NORRIS IMPRINT

 hello@abholton.com

 @A.B._Holton

# You May Also Like ...

AFTER HEARTBREAK SHATTERED her first marriage, Harper found unexpected love with Miles, a devoted billionaire entrepreneur. But when betrayal, temptation, and doubt threaten their bond, will their love survive? In this gripping tale of love, loyalty, deception, and healing. Find out if Harper and Miles can weather the storm or if their once-perfect world will come crashing down.

IN 199 DATE IDEAS The Ultimate Guide to Keeping the Spark Alive, couples rediscover dating as the key to emotional intimacy and relationship strength. Featuring over 200 creative ideas from adventurous outings to cozy nights. This guide inspires partners at any stage to rekindle love, deepen connections, and keep the spark alive for a lifetime.

HER LAUGHTER IS contagious, her smiles are as bright as the stars, and her spirit of love lights up every corner of their lives. Perfect for bedtime reading or any moment you want to feel wrapped in the warmth of family, Lily, Our Little Light will remind readers of all ages of the small wonders that make life truly luminous.